Jamestown, Alaska

Also by Frank Turner Hollon

The Pains of April

The God File

A Thin Difference

Life Is a Strange Place

The Point of Fracture

Glitter Girl and the Crazy Cheese

blood and circumstance

The Wait

Austin and Emily

The Book of Neil

To Jeff Beard, Jr.

I hope you like the book!

Jamestown, Alaska

a novel

Frank Turner Hollon

DZANC BOOKS

5220 Dexter Ann Arbor Rd.
Ann Arbor, MI 48103
www.dzancbooks.org

Library of Congress Cataloging-in-Publication Data

Names: Hollon, Frank Turner, 1963- author.
Title: Jamestown, Alaska : a novel / by Frank Turner Hollon.
Description: First Edition. | Ann Arbor, MI : Dzanc Books, 2016.
Identifiers: LCCN 2015033330 | ISBN 9781938103506 (paperback)
Subjects: | BISAC: FICTION / Satire. | FICTION / Humorous. |
GSAFD: Mystery
fiction.
Classification: LCC PS3608.O494 J36 2016 | DDC 813/.6--dc23
LC record available at http://lccn.loc.gov/2015033330

First US edition: June 2016
ISBN: 978-1-938103-50-6
Book design by Michelle Dotter

Printed in the United States of America

10 9 8 7 6 5 4 3 2 1

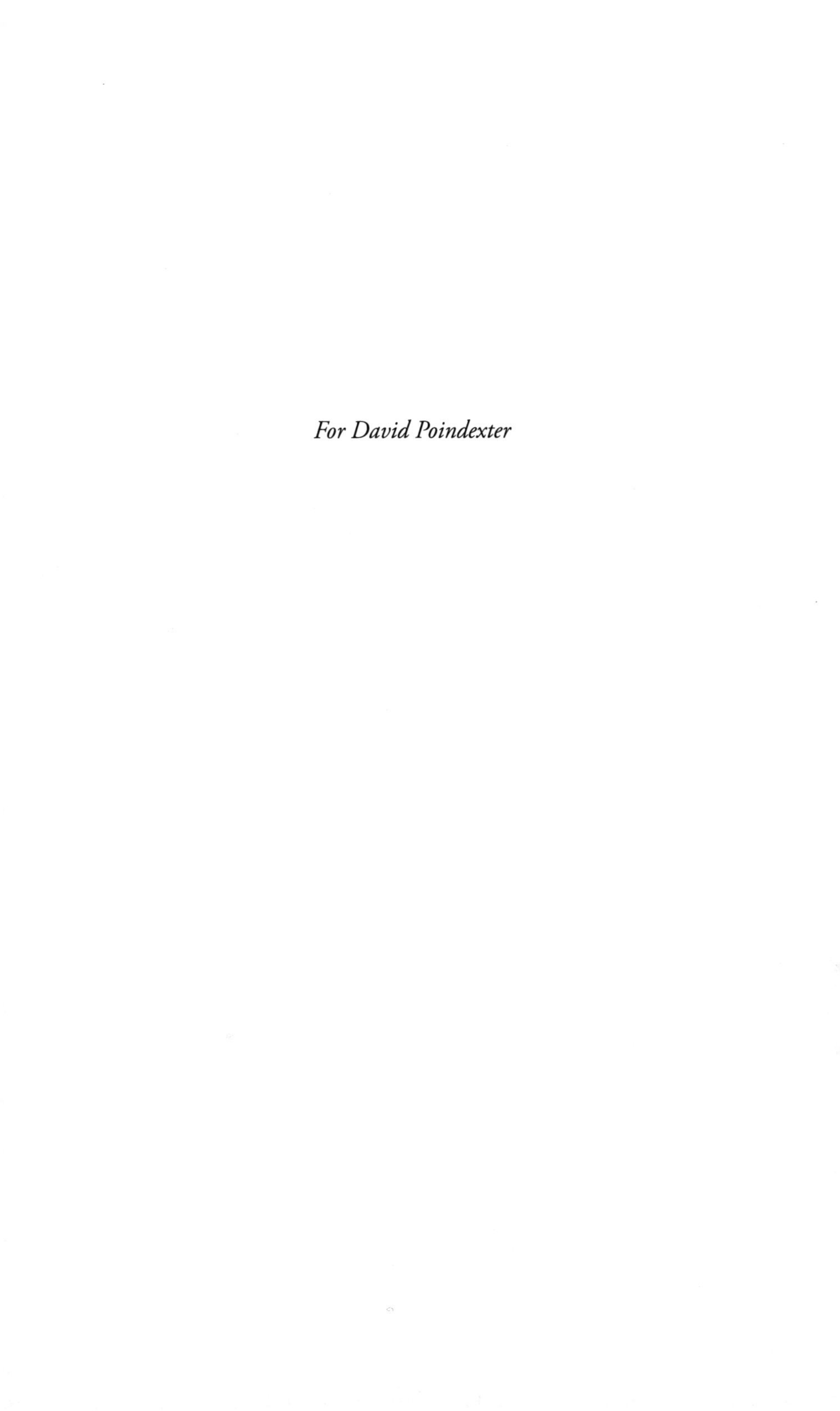

For David Poindexter

The three things you can't fake are
erections, competence, and creativity.

—Douglas Copeland

THE EXPLANATION

The old people each generation say, "The world has gotten crazier and crazier. Crime. Mental illness. Drug addicts. Child molesters. Alcoholics. Ungodliness. Obesity. Laziness. Folks just don't treat each other like they did when I was growing up."

And the young people say, "That isn't true. We just see much more of it now on television and the Internet. We're constantly bombarded by the bad things. The same bad things that always existed since the beginning of mankind. But the world, the human race, isn't actually in decline. It just seems that way. Really.

"And by the way, shut up, Grandma."

It was April. My daughter, Sara, sat next to me at the kitchen table in front of her cereal. A new brand of cereal that never got soggy. It would remain crispy even if left floating in a bowl of lukewarm milk for six months in a hot garage. The milk would sour, of course, but the cereal would always be crunchy. At least that's what the commercial promised.

I was reading the newspaper. There was an article about a twenty-one-year-old woman and her twenty-three-year-old boyfriend who killed the woman's three-year-old child in Texas. They admitted to burning her stomach with cigarettes, slamming the little girl's head against the wall, and kicking her repeatedly until she died. The child was found buried face down in a muddy shallow grave behind a trailer park still wearing her Little Mermaid nightgown. She had three skull fractures, bruises all over her body, and more than fifty cigarette burns.

I remember thinking, "I don't believe anymore that everything will be all right. I don't believe in people anymore. The world is fucked up just like the old people say."

It was only the beginning. The proverbial tip of the iceberg. The twenty-one-year-old woman and the twenty-three-year-old man didn't deserve to live another minute. There was no need for explanations or evaluations, no need to blame methamphetamines, or a bad childhood, or the educational system, or chemical preservatives in our cereal.

The strongest natural-born instinct in a human, besides self-preservation, is caring for our children. The further we become separated from nature, the further we fall.

I remember looking over at Sara sitting quietly. She was six. Her red book bag hung on the back of her chair. She was everything good about life. Young, soft, with bright blue eyes and her hair pulled into a ponytail. She looked up when she saw me watching her, and I was struck by the gentle lines and simple beauty of a child's face, the obligation of youth. It was a crystal moment for me. As clean and clear as any I've ever had before or since.

I don't know exactly what made me say it. I'd like to believe it was God; regardless I said, "I won't leave you in a world like this, Sara. I won't just complain. I'll do something to change it. I promise."

She rolled her eyes like I was a two-headed idiot and made a low, groaning sound above her breakfast. A sound I would expect to come from a badger.

It's difficult sometimes not to believe in fate. Two days after my promise to Sara, someone left a small book on my front doorstep. It was dark red, the color of dried blood, with no title or author's name embossed on the hardcover. It fit neatly in my hand.

Standing on the doorstep, I felt a draft of cool morning air blow up my robe as I bent over to pick up the book. I was wearing no underwear, of course, and hoped to go the entire day with such freedom.

Inside were these words:

The Survival Manifesto

I

In the beginning, there was something. And that something, once it came to exist, existed to survive. Survival is the greatest natural force in the history of the universe.

In nature, only the strongest, smartest, most capable survive. The weak perish, the herd culled daily, the weaker members eaten by predators, susceptible to disease, unable to feed themselves. This serves two purposes. First, with each death the herd immediately becomes stronger as a unit. There are more resources for the surviving members, and those that survive are not compromised by the need to oversee the welfare of the incompetent, to spend time and energy protecting or providing for dependent members.

Secondly, the DNA of the weaker individual is eradicated. Lazy, dimwitted, or egotistical members of the community who are genetically incapable of properly raising offspring, or whose offspring may be inherently incompetent, are removed from the gene pool, and therefore the herd continues to improve with each generation.

This law of survival of the fittest is fundamental to the continuation of each individual species since the beginning of all time.

II

The human species evolved under God's natural law, thriving and prospering, becoming stronger, smarter, and more capable. Population growth and intelligence led to civilization, and the very definition of civilization encompasses the manner in which the weak are treated. Each culture around the world, as they passed through the levels of becoming civilized, devised support systems for the members of the species previously sacrificed under natural law.

The sick, handicapped, and infirm were provided health care, medicine, and shelter. The lazy were given government assistance, welfare, subsidized housing, and free food. The immoral, thieves, murderers, and child molesters were housed in prisons, fed, and provided shelter and essentials. Drug addicts and alcoholics were provided rehabilitation, alternative drugs, and job placements. The mentally ill were given a lifetime of medicines and residential care.

Providing for these people seemed to make perfect sense. After all, we, as a species, had progressed so successfully and so quickly through God's natural laws that the competent, moral, hardworking people outnumbered the weak and needy tenfold. There were ten competent, ethical, hardworking adults who needed only to provide for themselves and their children, for every one individual who could not, or would not, provide for himself.

III

Generations passed and the support systems in the cultures around the world began to feel the weight of their enormous burden. Entire countries and continents struggled with the idea of who should get what and how much.

Governments were overthrown. Wars were waged. The strong often spilled the blood of the strong, while the weak, incompetent, and immoral waited impatiently for the bounty, their hands outstretched.

It became sacrilegious to denounce the lazy, the addicted, the obese, the prostitutes, adulterers, thieves, liars, or the mentally ill. Governments around the world became a refuge of shame, and the incompetent continued to breed at an alarming rate, twice or more the rate of the moral and hardworking. After all, the moral and hardworking understood through education the financial obligation of additional children, and understood birth control, and remained sober and rational as they worked their eight, ten, twelve-hour days to provide for themselves, their children, and those who could not, or would not, work.

The lazy, incompetent, and immoral were incapable of raising their children to be hardworking, competent, and moral. They could not instill in their children a strong work ethic, a moral foundation, or a true appreciation of God and this world. Further complicating the situation was degraded DNA traveling unchecked from generation to generation, helping to insure the rapid proliferation of the weakest members of the human species around the globe.

Eventually, the percentages began to shift. Soon, there were only seven hardworking, independent, and moral people for every one dependent individual waiting for his government check to arrive, or demanding free services from doctors and lawyers, or sitting around watching television in squalor wondering why anyone would complain about tax increases.

And then there were five to every one. And then only three. The burden itself became immoral. The mantra of the incompetent was, "Something for nothing," and the providers were blackmailed by their own morality into believing they were wrong to question the burden. Wrong to want what they earned.

IV

The further you stray from nature, the further you stray from God. The human species has proven this point once again. When the elders of each generation the past three hundred years insisted their world was becoming worse, they were right. Protecting the weak from the consequences of nature is exactly what God intended to guard against, and the results of the failure are monumental.

The competent choose education. The incompetent choose to quit. The competent choose to work hard every day, rain or shine, to provide food and a safe home for their children. The incompetent sleep late and get fired again, blame everyone else for their failures, and expect charity. The competent would rather have five dollars they earned instead of ten dollars for free. They'd go hungry before they would steal. They'd suffer before they would lie. The incompetent don't understand the difference and never will.

"Something for nothing," we hear in a whisper. And pretty soon it is no longer whispered, but yelled with entitlement.

It is one thing to ask a hardworking man to dig a ditch while another man stands and watches. It is a different thing to ask the hardworking man to dig the ditch, and then, when he receives his compensation, force him to split his pay with the man who merely watched.

Recently, society has taken this shame to a new level. The hardworking man is not only forced to share his compensation, he is told it is right. He is told it is moral. He is told it is civilized.

Every revolution in the history of the world started with two people. One speaking, and one listening.

V

Identifying the problem is simple and obvious. Identifying the cause of the problem isn't nearly as simple or obvious, and the solutions appear to be draconian at best.

Do we backtrack, cull the herd of all those members nature would have culled if left alone?

Do we force chemical castration and contraceptive devices on the incompetent and the children of the incompetent, to end the cycle in one generation?

Do we cease supporting and providing for those who will not and cannot provide for themselves after we have enabled the inept to exist?

Do we simply forge ahead and wait for the Apocalypse?

Maybe, for those of us who have no children or grandchildren, the end is in sight. For the rest of us, doing nothing is no longer an option. If we are to follow the laws of nature and God, then we must choose our children over everything. We must provide for them first, and providing includes leaving them a world, or at least a small part of the world, worthy of life.

We must start over.

VI

Our technology does not allow us to move to another planet. We cannot relocate to the moon or underground. Instead, we must choose a place on Earth relatively unpopulated, with vast natural resources, defendable borders, and access to the world's oceans.

Antarctica is too harsh and cold. The world's deserts are virtually unlivable for a large population. There are now over seven billion people crawling around the planet eating up resources faster than they can be replenished, building cities upon cities, and polluting everything they touch. The Earth has perhaps been irreparably damaged. Clean water and food have become rare commodities. Nowhere we choose to go will be far enough away. Our future homeland will forever be affected, directly or indirectly, by those we leave behind. In fact, when they recognize their providers have ceased to provide, that we are no longer influenced by their demands for sympathy and charity, conflict is inevitable, and we shall be prepared.

Alaska.

586,412 square miles. One-fifth the size of the continental United States. 33,904 miles of shoreline bordering the north Pacific Ocean, Bering Sea, Chukchi Sea, and Arctic

Ocean. 39 mountain ranges. 3,000,000 lakes, including 94 with surface areas in excess of ten square miles. 3,000 rivers, and 1,800 named islands.

The population is relatively small and can be controlled and segregated. The islands can be utilized for defense purposes. The climate is tolerable, food sources vast, and natural resources still relatively plentiful. As a state associated with the United States of America, access to Alaska is simple. The political and bureaucratic institutions can be manipulated as necessary to allow our entrance, and subsequently manipulated to close the borders.

VII

Although the logistics of the entire plan are obviously immense, perhaps the most difficult decision entails who will or will not be allowed to participate.

Race shall not be a determining factor. Religion shall not be a determining factor. Country of origin, degree of skin pigmentation, sexual preference, hair or eye color, height or weight, sex, wealth, or age shall never be determining factors.

The desire and compulsion to work hard is universal and fundamental to everything.

Those who will not work hard shall be excluded.

Rapists, child molesters, pornographers, prostitutes, and those who commit adultery shall be excluded.

Those dependent upon alcohol or drugs shall be excluded.

Those afflicted with mental illness shall be excluded.

Liars, thieves, spouse abusers, and murderers shall be excluded.

Those who disrespect animals, children, or the environment shall be excluded.

Those who cast blame, refuse responsibility, and wallow in self-pity shall be excluded.

Any other immoral, unethical, or dependent individual may be excluded at our discretion.

Anyone who works hard is acceptable regardless of physical limitations.

The elderly and infirm are acceptable if they lived lives of self-sufficiency and independence.

All children under five are acceptable regardless of DNA.

We determine who is, or who is not, acceptable, and invitations are extended or revoked at our discretion.

VIII

Someone must decide.

Someone, or a group of people, must make the difficult decisions if we are to salvage a decent world and a decent life for ourselves, our children, and our children's children.

The Committee shall consist of seven.

Each member has a single vote.

A writer shall be recruited to document the entirety of the revolution in a book to be handed down from generation to generation in the homeland.

The most competent doctors, craftsmen, carpenters, scientists, engineers, lawyers, mechanics, teachers, artists, musicians, pilots, veterinarians, soldiers, religious leaders, laborers, farmers, comedians, secretaries, bankers, college professors, etc., shall be identified and recruited, along with their immediate families.

Those who accept the invitation shall migrate systematically to the new homeland over a period of years, based on the necessity of each individual in the creation of the framework of the new society. Those not invited will be left to their own means of survival the way nature intended. Eventually, those competent people who choose not to participate shall be crushed under the weight of the beggars. The government checks shall cease to arrive in the mailbox. The grocery store shelves will be empty. The electricity, phone service, garbage pick-up, cable TV, Internet access, hot water, and everything else provided previously by the hardworking, moral, and competent shall disappear, and chaos shall rule as the herd culls itself through the violence of deprivation.

IX

The best of the best shall plan our defense on land and sea.

The best of the best shall harvest our fields, plan our cities, protect our borders, control immigration, teach our children, protect our resources, fish our waters, design our justice system, ensure fresh clean water, build our homes, manage our banks, run our offices, care for our sick, write our novels, compose our music, and everything else we desire.

Those who refuse to work hard shall be expelled permanently.

Those who rape or molest children shall be expelled permanently.

Those who abuse drugs or alcohol shall be expelled permanently.

Those who steal, lie, cheat, demand something for nothing, murder, or defile shall be expelled permanently.

The Committee shall make all decisions the way decisions should be made, with purity of conscience based upon the facts at hand and the laws of nature. The only capital offenses shall be the distortion of our history by those who document such things, or the compromise of our values by a member of the Committee.

There will be no need for welfare programs, government assistance, food stamps, health insurance, appointed attorneys, child welfare or unfair taxes.

There will be no need for prisons. Nature will solve the problem upon expulsion. The world outside our borders will be unsafe and vile, exactly as we allowed it to become, and although perhaps the meek, those deficient in spirit and courage, have inherited the Earth temporarily, it is the strong, those chosen by God, who will and must survive.

X

As the world outside our homeland deteriorates and erodes and our internal population grows and flourishes, ultimately we must begin the process of expansion. We shall stretch outside our borders one mile at a time to secure additional lands, clearing each square mile of humans, poisons, and waste.

Greed and power shall not factor into the decisions of expansion or the rate of such expansion. Time is our ally. Nature will do most of the difficult work for us.

Eventually, the entire planet will be cleared of the debris, and the human species will continue its progress as intended.

The cycle shall never repeat itself. The lessons we have learned shall be passed from adult to child, and these lessons will be taught to the children through realistic living examples, one generation at a time, to ensure mankind will never again consciously decide to violate the ultimate law of nature, bringing hardship, ruin, and dishonor upon the people of this great planet.

Never again.

God Bless Alaska.

I first read the book sitting in my white bathrobe alone on my back porch. The kids had already gone to school. My wife was in a meeting for one of her many well-meaning civic clubs. The house was remarkably quiet, or at least seemed that way as I read the small book from start to finish, and then read it again.

There was no author's name, no contact information, no ISBN number or anything else to identify the source. I was familiar with the publishing business. At the time, I was writing my ninth novel full time out of my home. I was one of the lucky few who stumble into financial success in the book business, and finally, after the fifth published novel, I'd quit my job and taken the leap of faith.

I searched for "Survival Manifesto" on the Internet. Nothing. I called my editor.

"Susan, have you ever heard of a little book called *The Survival Manifesto*?"

"No. How's the new novel comin' along, Aaron?" she asked.

"Fine. It's a small book, like a handbook, dark red. It's high-quality paper."

"Who's the publisher?"

"It doesn't say. There's no author's name. Nothing on the spine."

"I don't know," she said. "Are you more than half-finished? We won't have a problem with a publication date next spring, will we?"

"No, Susan, we won't."

Our conversations always led me to believe she was smack in the middle of something more important than me, like maybe a doughnut, but it was just her way. Truthfully, my productivity was essential to her success, and we both knew it. Snappy titles. Crisp repetition. Churn, churn, churn.

I sat back down on the porch and read the book again for a third time. It made me feel peculiar, like somebody was watching me, and I walked around the house peeking out windows at the neighborhood street. I even opened the front door and stood outside looking for anyone out of place, anyone who might have watched when I picked up the little book off the welcome mat. The cool breeze rediscovered my privates. Mr. Matson across the street looked up from his flowerbed and watched me curiously over the top of his glasses.

My wife came home midmorning, sharply dressed and busy as usual.

"Michelle, did you see anyone put anything by the front door?" I asked.

"No. Did I get a package?"

"It was a book."

"One of your books?" she asked.

"No. A little red book."

I peeked out the front window again. Mr. Matson was digging a tiny hole in his yard. I watched him dig.

My wife said, "Don't forget Brad's baseball practice tonight. And don't forget Sara's soccer game. It starts at seven. I've got a supper meeting at Rita Blanchard's house. It's for all the wives in the neighborhood. I think she wants to get the neighborhood committee to cut down the trees in the median in front of her house. I don't think we should. Personally, I like those trees. What do you think?"

"I think we should have unbridled intercourse in the laundry room," I suggested.

"Don't be silly," she said, without malice.

I didn't feel much like writing. The words of the little red book still floated inside my mind in a warm broth. I felt myself thinking about lunch. Thinking about anything except the prospect of sitting at my desk in front of an empty sheet of paper.

"Why's that silly?" I asked, our conversation scripted.

"I'm gonna leave you alone to write, honey," she said. It was something she said a lot. I had no more interest in where she went than she had in what I wrote. It was a job, and eight novels later I'd gotten good at it. I actually still enjoyed writing sometimes but not on this particular day. On this particular day I didn't feel much like doing anything. I watched my wife back out of the driveway in her grey BMW, going wherever she went when she said she was leaving me alone to write.

Standing in the shower after my wife left, the ideas from the red book wouldn't leave me alone. Fragments had existed in my mind, but separate, unconnected to one another. Nagging thoughts free-floated through the lives of fictitious characters in my books or underneath conversations with strangers. But never had I demanded or allowed the fusion of these fragments into such a dangerous and rude ideology.

I considered the possibility that my editor had delivered the book for the purpose of sparking my creativity. Her fear of my imagination drying up and us missing the next deadline was enough to push the woman to new measures.

More likely was the possibility a prospective writer wanted my opinion. Ever since my third book landed on the bestsellers list, closet writers approached me everywhere asking the same questions over and over. It seemed everyone in the world considered themselves a writer in waiting, simply waiting for the perfect moment to put pen to paper and create a work of pure genius.

I found myself venturing out of the house less and less. I would be handed manuscripts at church, given handwritten short stories at the ballpark, or recited lengthy narratives about crazy uncles at the gas station. I was the closest thing we had to a celebrity in our little town, with the possible exception of Grady Cumberland, who played professional football one season before he blew out a knee. I forget who he played for.

I finally decided I'd figured out the mystery of the little red book. Someone had self-published and wanted my encouragement to write the fleshed-out version. I'd probably get approached in the grocery store by some hyperactive little maniac holding an identical, blood-red book, watching my every move in the vegetable aisle.

I put the white robe back on, still naked underneath, and poured myself a third cup of coffee. Truthfully, I wasn't in the middle of my next novel. I'd started and stopped three different times with three different ideas I hated. It wasn't really writer's block, but instead, writer's boredom. I worked very hard at not trying to figure it out too much.

I peeked through the front window again. All clear. I'd left the little red book on the back porch, and my body moved in that direction like a slow robot until I stood in the open doorway between the living room and the screened-in porch, staring at the trampoline in the backyard.

To my right, in the far corner of my vision, something didn't belong. A form where a form hadn't been. A color out of sequence with the colors of the cushions on the wicker couch and chairs.

My head turned slowly. There was a man in my house sitting casually in my chair and wearing a maroon sweater, his legs crossed.

It took a moment for my eyes to see what they saw and another moment for my mind to register it. I screamed involuntarily and spilled most of my coffee. It was a high-pitched, girlish scream, and along with the fear of having a strange man in my house, I was instantly embarrassed I'd released such a sound.

The man didn't move. He just sat there. A white man, medium build, maybe late forties early fifties, khaki pants, not quite smiling, with sandy-grey hair and a mild expression on his tan face.

"Who are you?" I said sharply.

With the proper hesitation, he simply answered, "Bryan."

Of course, at the time, I didn't know how to spell his name, and for unknown reasons, even in the face of such an unusual situation, I wondered if it was spelled with a "y" or an "i."

"Is that spelled with a 'y' or an 'i'?" I asked.

"Y," he answered.

It was almost like we were friends—like he stopped by nearly every morning and sat in the same chair, and we sipped coffee and talked about the same things people talk about. It's hard to explain now.

At the man's elbow, resting on the table next to the lamp, was the little red book. It was nearly the same color as the man's sweater, but not quite. Just a shade off.

"Have a seat," Bryan offered.

I said, "Maybe I should get my gun and shoot you dead in my house, whoever you are."

He tried not to smile.

"You don't own a gun, Aaron."

He was right, of course. I didn't own a gun. I'd never owned a gun in my life. I remained standing in the doorway, the jolt of panic subsiding slowly.

"Did you write the book?" I asked, nodding in the direction of the table. I figured maybe he was the wannabe writer freak I expected to encounter in the grocery store, only

with a unique approach. Breaking and entering. Scaring the shit out of people before delivering his sales pitch.

He looked over at *The Survival Manifesto.*

"Oh, no," he said, and finally smiled outright. "Not me."

"Did you put it on my doorstep?" I asked.

"Yes, guilty as charged."

He was very calming. His hands remained in sight at all times. His body rested against the back of the chair, one leg crossed over the other, and he held eye contact, but it wasn't intimidating. Again, it was almost like we'd sat together for hours at a time, shared conversations about those things that require two people to look into each other's eyes. He wasn't at all like the little hyperactive wannabe writer I expected.

"Aren't you afraid I'll call the police?" I said.

"No," he answered. And he didn't seem to be at all.

"You're not the first person to show up at my doorstep wanting me to provide some magical insight into writing the next great American novel, you know."

"I don't imagine so, if that's what I was here for. But that's not why I'm here."

I took a sip from my coffee cup. It was nearly empty.

"It's an interesting book, isn't it?" he asked.

"I wouldn't know," I said. "I didn't read it."

He smiled again. "Yes, you did. More than once."

He was sure of himself, but not in a cocky way, patient and rational.

"How did you get in here?" I asked.

"The back door was unlocked. I knocked, but no one answered."

"Maybe that's because I didn't want anyone in my house."

"Maybe," he said. "But maybe it's because you were in the shower."

We came to a standstill. It was time for him to say what he came to say, and it was my turn to be patient.

He asked, "What did you think of the book?"

I looked again out into the backyard. It was a beautiful clear day. The grass around the trampoline was a faded green except for one worn spot. It was the spot Sara and Brad always landed when they climbed down. Brad would sometimes fly through the air and come down hard on unbreakable legs, like Spiderman. Something to see.

"It was entertaining. Not very realistic or feasible, but entertaining," I said.

The man looked at me like he knew exactly what I would say. Like perhaps, somewhere years ago, in another city on another back porch, he had given the same answer to the same question, and now he was the one to explain.

"What if I told you, Aaron, that it was happening as we speak? What if I told you it's not only possible, but it's actually happening, and for the past five years some of the most competent, hardworking, intelligent people in this world have been making these ideas a reality?"

I leaned my shoulder against the doorframe.

He continued, "As you can imagine, there are some extremely wealthy and powerful people interested in the possibilities. We've purchased huge tracts of land in Alaska under different names. We've managed to have our candidates elected to helpful positions. The infrastructure of the original city is being built. Men and their families are there now."

I purposefully didn't speak, suppressing the questions lining up one behind the other.

"It's not just an idea, Aaron. It's one of the most important things to happen to mankind in recorded history."

I took another sip of my coffee to create the impression of indifference and to give myself a moment to think. He watched me closely.

"What exactly are you doing here?" I asked.

He seemed to consider the question a positive sign.

"Well, you have the ability to communicate effectively and efficiently with the written word. This ability is underappreciated in our world of technology. It's rare and extremely important.

"In your novels there's an undercurrent of many of the ideas and issues contained in the *Manifesto.* Even though you've written your mystery novels as the marketplace dictates, underneath, they're really stories of people like you and me struggling with the frustrations of an impotent world.

"After all, we might make our fortunes off the idiots, but this is no place to raise our children, is it? We read about it in the newspaper every day. We hear it on television. Ridiculous, violent wars in countries that can't feed their people but can somehow afford machine guns. Children molested and abused every minute of every day in every corner of the world. It's a sick place, and we made it sick, Aaron. You and me and the rest of the hardworking, competent, moral people of the world who didn't pay attention to God's natural laws. And since we created the problem, it's our problem to solve. Wouldn't you agree?"

Bryan leaned up in his chair, not in a threatening manner, but as if pulled forward by his convictions. His voice was not pleading or demanding, it was very matter-of-fact, the way a teacher might explain mathematical absolutes.

I spoke. "Like I said, this is entertaining, but I'm not sure what it has to do with me. I've got work to do. Why don't you go sit in somebody else's house?"

"You've been chosen to write our history, Aaron. I was sent to extend an invitation for you to be our writer, the person who documents everything. It's extremely important for the human race to learn from our mistakes so they're not repeated throughout history, over and over. What we're starting now, purging the world, will take many years and be excruciatingly difficult. It should only be done once. It should never be necessary again."

I was being recruited. For a fleeting moment I felt proud of being chosen, but in the next moment my skepticism returned. My stomach felt empty and hot. I thought about sitting down and decided against it.

I said, "So let me make sure I understand. You want me to accept this invitation, sell my house, stop writing novels, take my kids out of school, tell my wife she can't belong to the Neighborhood Wives' Club, and move to a new perfect world in Alaska to write the history of your cult? Is that it? Do I have it about right? How do I even know the place exists?"

"I'll take you there," he said.

"Is there something the matter with you, Bryan? Do you have medication you need to take or something? Because this isn't normal, you know? Showing up on my back porch, dressed all nice and neat, asking me to pack up, move to Alaska with a super-race of worker bees. It's weird, Bryan. Weird."

The man leaned back in his chair slowly. We looked at each other a moment in silence. There was no coffee left to sip.

He said, "Imagine the courage it took for those men, women, and children to climb aboard the Mayflower in 1620 to go to a new world, a place it would take them more than a month to reach across an endless ocean in a wooden boat, and if by a miracle they arrived, there would be no one to greet them. No stores or towns or schools. They didn't know if it would be cold or hot, rainy or dry, livable or full of enemies. Hell, Aaron, they didn't even know for sure the place existed. All they knew is they couldn't stay where they were. And so they packed a bag, held their children's hands, and climbed aboard to start over in a new world."

The way he told the story, I was there. Standing on the dock with Sara, looking up at the ship, her little hand in mine. The apprehension was like a wave over me. I could almost hear the slow groan of the boat drifting from the dock.

"Imagine the courage that took. The pure faith," he said.

I let my mind believe it for a second, but my words remained cynical.

"It can't work," I said. "Just think about all the problems with deciding who goes and who doesn't, the backlash from all the established countries when you take away their best and brightest. The logistics of the whole thing. It's just not possible. Sorry."

"Really? That's what they said to those people who climbed aboard the Mayflower. And even four hundred years ago, with none of the knowledge and technology we possess today, they became the foundation of the greatest country in the history of the Earth. The most freedom. The most opportunity. The most possibility. It's the same thing, Aaron. Except it won't take us hundreds of years. We can do it in a few generations. Brad and Sara's children will never know the immorality, the victimization, the fear, the disgust of this world that now exists. Because it simply won't exist. Not for us. And down the road, not at all, ever again."

Neither of us moved or broke eye contact. He waited and I waited, maybe both of us unsure what we waited for, and time passed, maybe thirty full seconds.

I finally said, "I think you should leave now."

He didn't seem surprised by my words and moved forward in the chair to stand. I watched him walk to the back door.

The man turned to face me. For the first time I could see he was tall. Taller than me by a few inches, but hunched over a little, fighting gravity.

"If you want to talk again, Aaron, we will. If you don't, we won't."

I watched him open the door and walk out into the backyard, past the trampoline. He hesitated for a moment on the worn spot in the grass, sliding his shoe across the hard dirt. The same spot Sara would stand and pull herself up. The same spot Brad would land with his unbreakable bare feet after flying through the blue sky.

He didn't look back. It was creepy.

When I was a small child, my parents thought I might be autistic. I didn't like crowds or loud noises. I refused to speak at all until my third birthday. I've always been obsessed with time and numbers, and my eyesight and hearing are far above average, but when it comes to people, I'd almost always rather be alone.

When Bryan left my house, I waited before I sat down. I wanted time to pass before I reacted to his intrusion into my life. The violation and insecurity mingled quietly with a low hum of excitement. Almost a sexual excitement.

Maybe he was just another wannabe freak writer carrying his whole storyline to the extreme. He wanted a blurb from me for the back cover for his doomsday bestseller. Probably a college professor, or maybe even a hired actor playing the part while the author sat in the car down the street biting his fingernails, listening to our conversation through a hidden microphone.

But I knew it wasn't so. I was being recruited to write, or rewrite, the history of a planned worldwide revolution. Not a revolution of the have-nots against the haves, or the blacks versus the whites, or even the Catholics against the Protestants. No, this revolution was even more powerful. They had God on their side, and Mother Nature, and history—or at least they believed they did, which was even scarier.

If it was true, good or bad, it was an amazing idea. Really a combination of other ideas, like the fragments I alluded to earlier, coming together to form a new fingerprint, a new possible direction and identity for the entire world.

My bowels began to move. I looked at the clock knowing it would be within a few minutes of 11:00 a.m., the time each morning my bowels decided to move, because they, my bowels, just like my brain, had an obsession with time, and were somehow able to know it was 11:00 a.m.

I took the newspaper with me. SHOOTER KILLS 12 IN MALL. Twelve people shopping for God knows what, gunned down by a nineteen-year-old, bushy-headed outcast wearing all black. He killed himself at the end of the tirade, blowing his brains across the sunglasses display.

The guy left a note telling the world he did what he did because he was mad about being fired from his menial job and not having a girlfriend. He was mad about getting kicked out of high school for no good reason, and hating his mother's new boyfriend, and not having a nicer car. Lastly, and perhaps most telling, the guy was mad about his bushy hair. The letter went on and on about how he prayed to have straight hair every night and woke up every morning with the same bushy hair on his head. Standing in front of the mirror, disbelieving. Bushy, bushy, bushy.

And so, somehow, this guy came to the decision to smuggle a rifle into the mall under his jacket, stand in a particular strategic spot, and shoot to death twelve people who had nothing to do whatsoever with getting him fired from his job, or his hair, or introducing his lovely mother to her lovely new boyfriend.

I couldn't help but imagine what Bryan would say. If not for three hundred years of coddling, this nineteen-year-old defective human being wouldn't exist. His mother and her boyfriend probably wouldn't exist. The competent students at his high school wouldn't have endured the disruption he caused. His boss wouldn't have been in the position where he considered hiring such a person, much less forced to fire the misfit. And those twelve people, assuming they were twelve competent consumers, would have simply paid for their purchases and headed home without the distraction of a bullet exploding their heads.

I sat down in the same chair where Bryan sat earlier. Before I picked up the book, my eyes scanned the backyard. Was I under surveillance? Maybe it was no coincidence Mr. Matson was digging around in his front yard on this particular morning. Maybe he was one of "them." The head of the neighborhood secret Alaskan surveillance squad. Probably not.

I read the book again from start to finish. On the back of the last page a phone number was written in blue ink. It wasn't there before. I would have seen it.

Bryan must have written it. The phone number was the way I would be able to contact him if I wanted to "talk again," as he said before he left.

Unfortunately, by this point, I was unable to think of much else. One piece of the grand idea would grow to the next and my mind would circle between the existential and the practical. It was one thing to think such thoughts, another thing to truly believe them, and still something altogether different to attempt a massive revolt of the entire planet.

If there were madmen willing to try such a thing, it would be worth writing about. At least I let myself think so, for the sake of argument.

I stood on the sidelines of the soccer game with my hands in my pockets, watching Sara run up and down the field, seemingly at random. I'd never learned the rules of soccer. Baseball was my game, as you might imagine, organized within the framework of a million statistics. Soccer looked insane. Kids knocking over kids. Just by sheer probability, a ball would occasionally roll slowly into a net and one sideline or the other would erupt with euphoria.

I always stayed off to the side by myself. I simply could no longer endure the inane casual conversations with people I didn't know or particularly care about.

I thought I was in the clear until a short, balding man sidled up to me from behind. I pretended to be entranced by the soccer game. He spoke anyway. Arms crossed. Very serious. Man talk.

"You think it'll rain tomorrow?"

"I don't know."

"Weatherman says it's supposed to rain. We could sure use it." He looked up to the sky.

"Yeah."

"Say, what's it mean to be offsides in soccer anyway?"

"I'm not sure."

"I grew up playing football. Football's a man's game. I'm sure soccer's a good sport. I just don't know the rules."

Out of the corner of my eye, I watched his mouth move. It would stay open slightly between sentences. Paranoia crept inside me. My eyes searched across the field for the maroon sweater in the crowd of parents. Was the strange man to my left another Bryan, or was he just one more lonely person on the planet longing to talk nonsense to any stranger who wouldn't run away?

A redheaded girl on the other team stole the ball from Sara and took off down the sideline with my daughter just a few steps behind. The two girls were right in front of me. Sara had a determined look on her little face.

She kicked hard at the redheaded girl from behind, missing the ball and kicking her square in the side of the knee. The girl crumpled to the ground holding her leg, tears instantly streaming down her face.

I saw a man, redheaded himself, on the other side of the field take off toward us at full stride. His hands were both clenched into fists, and as he got closer I could see the anger hardened on his face.

"That little bitch," he yelled. "That little bitch tripped Marcie on purpose."

Spit flew from his mouth. I couldn't believe it was actually happening. I couldn't believe anyone would name their child Marcie.

The short, balding man melted away into the background. Sara retreated behind my leg. The adrenaline, nature's injection, rushed outward from my heart into every inch of my bloodstream, a raging river of energy.

The crazy man stormed past his child and we were face to face, veins in his forehead pulsing with every heartbeat. Bloodshot eyes sunk deep in his Cro-Magnon skull. Even before he spoke I could smell the alcohol seeping from his large pores, thick and heavy.

He was drunk. The man was actually drunk at his six-year-old daughter's soccer game. Intoxicated to the point of absurd violence, having made a conscious, rational choice to drink alcohol before the game like the rational choice the nineteen-year-old in the mall made to vindicate his unanswered prayers through the shooting of strangers.

With his yellow teeth clenched, the redheaded man said, "Is that your little bitch who tripped my daughter?"

Of course, the answer was, "Yes." We'd all seen it. Sara kicked her in the knee. Knocked her down. We all knew the answer to his question.

Without moving my head, I dropped my eyes to the little girl on the ground. She'd stopped crying. She was horrified by her father, and I could tell by the look on her face she'd seen it all before. Seen her father flying across rooms to shove her mother up against walls, his hand at her throat. Smelled the alcohol, seen the bloodshot eyes up close. Felt his anger in every bone of her transparent body.

I couldn't stop looking at her. The crazy man was two inches from my nose, but it was the little girl who held my attention. Somewhere inside her, deep down inside, she wanted me to kill the man. Shove a knife into his belly, sharp side up, and gut the motherfucker right there on the soccer field. Because somewhere inside her, she knew, as shocking as it might be to watch her father murdered in front of her eyes under the lights of a soccer game, it would save her mother and herself a lifetime of misery and brutality.

I could feel other people gathering. I could hear voices asking him to step away, but I couldn't lift my eyes from the girl.

People came between us. The spell was broken. The disgusting, drunk father was pulled away. I knelt to face Sara. Her eyes were full of tears, and when I wrapped my arms around her I could feel her fragile body shivering.

Late that night, alone on the porch, after three and half bourbon and Cokes, I called the phone number written in the back of the book. It rang and rang and rang. Finally, Bryan's voice asked me to leave a message.

I hung up without speaking and then fixed myself a sandwich.

According to Michelle, the Neighborhood Wives' Club meeting didn't go well. After dessert and coffee, the hostess, Rita Blanchard, made a motion for the club to expend funds on the removal of several trees in the median in front of her two-story house. The trees were dropping bothersome leaves and acorns as well as blocking the afternoon sun.

Cindy Sheerer, the doctor's wife, requested to be heard before the vote was taken. As she explained her love of trees in general and the beauty these particular trees added to the neighborhood, Rita Blanchard's puffy face became more and more red. Eventually, she lost her civility.

"You don't have to deal with a million acorns. Or those God-damned squirrels all over the roof."

Cindy held her ground.

"Rita, you knew the trees were there when you moved into this house. They're in the median, the common ground."

At this point, my wife, flush with the unbearable tension in the room, apparently said, "This pie is delicious."

"Fuck the pie," Rita Blanchard shouted. "I want the trees gone."

A hasty vote was taken, and despite Rita's hospitality hosting the dinner, she lost by a slim margin.

I woke up the next morning to the phone ringing.

"Hello."

"Aaron?"

"Yes," I answered, trying to get my bearings.

"This is Cindy Sheerer."

She was yelling.

"Why are you yelling?" I asked.

"My yard," she blurted out.

I handed the phone to Michelle.

"It's for you."

I could hear Cindy's voice. "My yard is full of acorns. That bitch dumped buckets of acorns in my yard in the middle of the night."

"Oh my God," my wife said.

In my mind I could see Rita Blanchard, wearing gloves and overalls, filling a basket full of brown and green acorns, quietly driving the basket down the street in the back of her SUV while the neighborhood slept peacefully, and then dumping the basket in the middle of the Sheerers' pristine lawn next to another mound of acorns. After all, if they were common-ground trees, then certainly the acorns were common-ground acorns. They should be shared with all.

When my wife drove away for the morning, I left the back door unlocked and took a long, slow shower. I held a faint hope Bryan would return so we could finish our conversation. Surely he had caller ID. He would know I'd called and hung up without leaving a message.

But the porch was empty. I sat down at the desk in my office at the end of the hall. I turned on my computer and pulled out a big yellow pad of paper and my favorite pen. I had a rule: never start writing a book unless I'm prepared to finish. This generally translated to months of thinking about ideas and taking notes before the first word appeared on top of the first page. But after my talk with Bryan, and the little red book, and the crazy man at the soccer game, I couldn't think of anything except the idea of starting the world all over again. And so I began taking notes on the yellow pad. Questions really. Things I wanted to ask Bryan. And before I knew it, I was sitting alone again late at night with the phone in my hand, dialing the number, this time sober.

Bryan's voice said calmly, "Leave a message, and I'll call you back."

I hung up. After all, what the hell was I doing? A complete stranger broke into my house. I had nothing, nothing besides the little red book, to support anything the man said.

Maybe I was desperate for something interesting to write about. Maybe I was sick of writing the same book with different names and different titles, the same formula. Blah, blah. Maybe my ego nibbled on the possibility I'd been chosen by the greatest people in the world to write the most important book since the Bible.

And then the next morning, after my shower, he was there. In the same chair, this time wearing a navy-blue sweater. I shuddered slightly, but remained calm, avoiding another squeal.

I stood in the doorway as before, in my robe, holding the same coffee cup.

"You called?" he said evenly.

I didn't want to appear too eager, so I just stood where I stood.

Bryan motioned with his hand, extending the invitation for me to sit across the coffee table from him, and this time I sat down, careful to cover my bare midsection.

We were quiet.

I wasn't sure where to start.

The man said, "The hottest places in Hell are reserved for those who, in times of great moral crisis, maintain their neutrality."

After he finished the sentence I said, "Is that your recruitment slogan?"

He smiled. "No, that's Dante Alighieri."

We were quiet again. I tried to think of the notes I'd written on the yellow pad.

Bryan leaned up in his chair. "I'm sure you have a lot of questions, Aaron. Most people do. Most of those questions you can answer for yourself, but why do you think, in the face of all the evidence around us, we try so hard to maintain this belief that everything will be all right if we just stand around and watch?"

I let him continue.

"Think about it. Just look around. Turn on the television. School shootings every week. Women and children disappearing from their homes. Bodies found scattered around the countryside. Does that sound all right to you?

"A complete breakdown of the family unit. Divorces. Children raised without fathers. Adultery is a big game. People break their vows to themselves, to God, like it was nothing.

"Pick up a magazine. Listen to the radio. People don't worship gods anymore.

They worship other people. Actors whose gift, at best, is speaking lines written by other people. TV preachers. Musicians. Athletes. The more immoral, drug-addicted, scandalous, egotistical, the more they're worshipped, lavished with our attention, our money.

"Does that sound all right to you?"

I leaned up in my chair also, and said, "Do you think you're the first person to spew the doomsday message? Do you think you're the first to scare the hell out of everybody, saying we have the misfortune of finding ourselves at the tail end of the human species?"

He liked the question, I could tell. He scooted up just a little farther in his chair.

"No, I don't. But there's a difference. We have a solution. Offering a solution, a real solution, isn't doomsday. It's the opposite."

I shot back, "Come on, Bryan, if that's really your name, can you imagine the multitude of problems with this Committee you talk about? The Neighborhood Wives' Club can't even decide whether to cut down a tree, and you propose a Committee of seven people will decide everything from who gets invited to who gets kicked out."

He said, "Nothing's perfect, Aaron. Nothing ever has been, and nothing ever will be. We'll make mistakes. We'll leave good people behind. But our cause is noble. It is the cause of mankind."

We looked at each other across the table.

"Is that another slogan?" I asked sarcastically.

Bryan smiled again. "No, that's George Washington."

"Really?" I asked.

"Really."

If he was an actor, he was good. If the guy was a wannabe writer desiring a blurb for his new book, he was the most dedicated wannabe writer in history. I could feel myself beginning to believe.

"Aaron, think about it. Why do we really put up with working so hard every day of our lives to provide food, housing, medical care, free legal services, free drug rehabilitation, and everything else for drug addicts, convicted felons, people who refuse to be educated, people who refuse to work, the immoral masses? Why?"

I lowered my head and thought about it. "I don't know."

"So they won't come into our neighborhoods, Aaron. Rape our wives, take our children, steal our TV sets, lie on our couches smoking cigarettes in our warm pajamas. So they'll stay in their shitty little trailers we provide, eat junk food, shoot up, use their pennies to buy a bottle of cheap liquor, a pack of generic cigarettes, and stay the hell away from us. That's why.

"We're not talking about lining people up against the wall and killing them. We're not talking about marching anybody to a gas chamber or poisoning their water. We're just talking about leaving. Letting nature decide who survives and who doesn't. Eliminating the underlying, unspoken daily threat that if we don't give them what they demand, they'll show up at our doorstep. Our new doorstep will be too far away, and we'll be protected by people just like me and you."

I leaned back slowly in my chair. I couldn't think of any more questions. He leaned back in his chair also, and we sat for a while like two guys who'd sat on the porch across from each other many times without speaking, eye to eye, until, without breaking eye contact and looking down, I noticed my robe had separated in the middle, exposing my penis between us.

It wasn't just slightly exposed. It was completely exposed. Absurd and surreal, suddenly naked from the waist down in the middle of a conversation with a man named Bryan.

I leaned up quickly and covered myself with a tug on the edge of the robe.

Did he think I'd done it on purpose? A test of some sort, maybe? A homosexual overture? Had he completely failed to notice my exposed genitalia? What now?

"Let me show you," he said.

"Show me what?" I managed to ask, afraid of the answer.

"Let me show you what we're doing in Alaska."

I looked at his face for any sign of embarrassment, any recognition of the uncomfortable situation. There was none. Maybe in Alaska, amongst the chosen people, it was quite normal for a person to expose their genitals casually during a friendly conversation.

He waited for an answer.

"Okay," I said, and to this day I wonder why I said such a thing.

Before he left, we agreed Bryan would pick me up two days later on Friday morning. I was to pack a week's worth of warm clothes and let him make all the travel arrangements.

I could still back out. Nothing was written in stone. I could call the phone number and leave a message saying I'd changed my mind. Maybe I was too busy on my new book. Or it just wasn't a good time to be traveling to Alaska to freeze my ass off.

But I knew I wouldn't call. The ideas were alive inside in my mind, and I felt the familiar irresistible pull I'd felt with each book before. Sometimes it started with the first thought. Sometimes I had to take notes or actually begin writing the first chapter, but each time the story would become bigger than me, stronger than me, and my mind would follow it out until the end. I'd written entire books, start to finish, that would never see an editor's desk or a bookstore shelf, but once I started I couldn't stop. I think they call it obsessive-compulsive disorder.

Bryan. Alaska. *The Survival Manifesto*. A worldwide secret. It was better than anything my imagination could conjure. I was tempted to write a few paragraphs, a summary, and send it to my editor so she'd know I wasn't just lying around the house in my robe sipping coffee. But I decided not to. What if she didn't like it? I'd keep the idea to myself, but I'd let her know I was traveling to Alaska to do some research for my next book. It would keep her content.

My wife came home while I was sitting on the porch alone thinking about things. At first she didn't see me, tiptoeing through the kitchen in her tennis outfit. Probably assuming I was down the hall in my office.

When she saw me she said, "What are you doing out here?"

My hands were in the pockets of my robe. I was sitting in the same place Bryan sat, and Michelle was standing in the doorway where I'd stood before.

"Have you ever thought about moving?"

A smile formed slowly on her face.

"Oh my God," she said. "The Davenports have a 'For Sale' sign in their yard. It's five thousand square feet with crown molding. It's even got a swimming pool."

"Five thousand square feet," I said. "Why would anyone need five thousand square feet?"

"What do you mean?" she asked.

We were at different ends of the conversation. I kept my hands in the pockets of my robe and leaned up in the chair.

"I mean, have you ever thought about moving away? Away from this town? Maybe somewhere like Canada?"

Her face changed. She thought about my question for a moment.

"No," she said. "I haven't. I don't know anybody in Canada."

And it was clear she was telling the truth. She'd never once, not even for a moment, considered moving far away to a place like Canada, or Alaska, or anywhere else.

"The publishing company is sending me to Alaska so I can research a few things for the book I'm working on."

"Alaska?" she repeated.

"Yeah. I go on Friday."

She turned and went back to the kitchen. I'd gone on research trips before. New York. Utah. An Indian reservation. One time I spent a week on a cattle ranch in south Texas. Ended up with chiggers.

I watched her remove a plastic bottle of water from the refrigerator and leave out the front door with her new tennis racket. I followed and watched Michelle through the dining-room window as she backed down the driveway and sped away.

Mr. Matson was standing at his mailbox across the street. He seemed to be staring directly at me, and continued to stare. I was quite sure he couldn't see anything through the blinds where I stood in the relative darkness of the dining room. But the man held his gaze like a statue.

This went on and on for an inordinate period of time, until I wondered if the man was dead, solidified upright on the way to the mailbox, the first person ever to die standing up and remain in such a position, until he finally moved. He opened the mailbox and placed what looked like a copy of the *The Survival Manifesto* inside, lifting the small flag on the side of the box.

I went to the porch. The little red book wasn't on the table where it had been before. I looked under the chair and around the back of the table to see if maybe it had fallen. No. It wasn't on my desk, or on the nightstand by the bed, or anywhere else I could see.

I called Michelle on her cell phone.

"Have you seen a little red book on the porch?"

"No." She was short. Probably still disappointed we wouldn't be buying the Davenports' five-thousand-square-foot house with a pool, where I could end up spending my life scooping leaves in a big blue net.

"Have you seen the book at all?" I asked.

"No," she said again, and then asked, "Are you having an affair, Aaron?"

"No," I answered. "No."

We were silent for at least five seconds.

"Good," she said, and hung up like everything was fine.

Bryan must have taken the book back. Was it my book I saw Mr. Matson put in his mailbox? Certainly not. He was just an old, retired, nosy neighbor, but I found myself camped out in the dining room reading the newspaper with my eyes fixed on the old man's mailbox.

The front page of the local paper had an article about a well-dressed man who made appointments with real estate agents to view expensive houses. While in the houses he would excuse himself to the bathroom, where he'd steal all the prescription medication and defecate in the tub. I thought of the Davenports' house. I thought of Eleanor Davenport pulling back the shower curtain to reveal the calling card of the well-dressed thief.

Out the window I watched the mailman pull up to the Matsons' house. He opened the box, removed something, and pushed down the flag. The mailman drove away and I started packing for Alaska, ignoring my paranoia while I matched socks and counted shirts.

The morning I was scheduled to leave, I sat as usual at the breakfast table with Sara while she methodically crunched her favorite cereal. It was always our best time to talk. Michelle was moving around the house performing routine tasks and Brad was perpetually late.

"Well, would you say so far you like kindergarten or you don't like kindergarten?"

"I don't like it today," she said.

"Why not?"

"Miss Simpson changed our seats yesterday. I have to sit next to George."

"What's wrong with George?" I asked.

"He's stupid," she answered.

I started to laugh and stopped myself. Sara took a large spoonful into her mouth and crunched.

"That's not a nice thing to say, Sara."

She finished chewing.

"Why not?" she asked seriously.

"Well, because we shouldn't say bad things about people."

Sara looked at me with great sincerity, like only a child can do. "That's just how God made him, Daddy. God made George stupid, and there's nothing we can do about it."

We sat at the table for a time, just me and my little girl.

"Would you like to move to Alaska?" I asked.

Without a missed beat, in perfect flow of the conversation, she said, "Will George be there?"

I smiled. "No, I don't think George will be there."

"Good," she said. "Then let's move to Alaska."

From the dining-room table I watched a car pull up in front of my house. It was black, four-door, and Bryan stepped out of the driver's side. He wore a grey sweater.

It was time to go.

THE JOURNEY

The inside of the black car smelled like Bryan. Clean, but not disinfectant or perfume. Like the smell of warm muffins.

The car was neat but not obsessively so. It was well worn, at least 100,000 miles. I could see a Miles Davis CD in the small space under the radio.

"I misplaced my book," I said.

Bryan buckled his seatbelt and said, "It's not your book, it's mine. I took it back on my second visit."

I'm not sure why, but I had a certain feeling I was making a huge mistake. I should be in my house with my wife and children instead of riding away from the neighborhood with this man. The thought formed in my brain, and almost, almost came out in words.

Before I could speak, Bryan said calmly, "You made a good decision, Aaron. There's nothing to lose. Just take a look, ask a few questions, talk to a few people. If you decide not to commit, just go back home and keep living your life. Like a test drive. No strings."

We rode in silence. A school bus stopped up ahead. It made me think of Sara and dumb George, and the kids in the kindergarten class beginning to slide gently into predetermined categories. Categories they may never escape.

"Where are we driving?" I asked.

"Well, we'll end up in Alaska. But we won't drive there, I promise."

He was purposefully vague.

"I'm not trying to be mysterious, but you're still an outsider, Aaron. There's a degree of secrecy until we reach a certain point. Obviously, we can't keep something like this completely secret, but after a certain point it doesn't matter, does it?"

He turned onto the interstate heading north.

"Have you ever done this before?" I asked.

"Done what?"

"Taken someone like myself on a recruiting tour."

Bryan smiled.

"No. You're my first."

"Why?"

"Because I selected you."

"Who are you to pick people to recruit?"

He said, "I'll answer that question later in the week."

"How did you get involved in all of this?" I asked.

He drove just above the speed limit. The sky was grey, but there was no feeling of rain, just greyness, and muffins.

"That's a fair question," he said. "I spent twenty years working in a juvenile court system. It provided me a special view of the decay at a very fundamental level.

"During those twenty years I was able to see the common denominator. Incompetent parents. Virtual idiots. People incapable of raising children. Incapable of teaching children the difference between right and wrong, good and bad, because the parents themselves don't know the difference.

"Around the eighteen year mark I figured out a few things I hadn't quite figured out. It goes much deeper, Aaron. It's like we talked about before. Lazy, stupid, unethical people not just allowed to survive, but subsidized, even encouraged.

"You just wouldn't believe it. Over and over and over again. Drug-addicted, unemployed, alcoholic, immoral, mentally ill parents sitting in the juvenile court system watching their lovely children fail out of school, abuse drugs, steal, lie, demand handouts, get pregnant.

"The cycle not only continues, it expands exponentially. It's amazing. In our society, we won't let people vote for the town mayor until they're eighteen. We won't let a college kid drink a cold beer until he's twenty-one. We won't let a minor under nineteen enter a contract, buy a car, or sign a lease, but anyone can have a baby. Any drunk, methamphetamine addict, violent criminal, uneducated, unemployed, retarded teenager, can screw on a mattress in the back room of a trailer, and they can have a child. A child you and I will financially support, who, because of some combination of DNA and intolerable environment, will kill you for your wallet if he gets a chance, or molest your little girl on the way home from the bus stop, or cut your wife's throat after raping her on your kitchen floor."

I could hear the anger in his voice, but it was a strong, controlled anger. A control that can only come from repetition or insanity, and I was beginning to think they might be the same thing.

He said, "And the rich parents weren't much better. They got angry that anyone would hold their children responsible. And you know why?"

"Why?"

"Because they didn't raise their children to survive. They raised their children to be dependent. It's easier. It feeds their egos. But it's contrary to nature. You cannot, as a parent, place yourself between your child and the repercussions of your child's actions. The lesson is very clear: do what you wish and never suffer the consequences. There's no need to work, money will be handed out regardless.

"And then those parents, some of them very competent, some who worked very hard for everything they have, cannot believe a judge, a police officer, a teacher would dare to hold their children accountable."

He wasn't wearing a wedding ring or other jewelry. The car held few clues.

"Were you a judge?" I asked.

He smiled again, but from the smile itself I couldn't tell if my question was ridiculous or directly on point.

"That's not important. Are you hungry?"

"Not really."

"Do you mind if I pull into this Burger King? I need to visit the men's room and get a little bite to eat so I can take my pill. I'll buy you a cup of coffee."

After his trip to the bathroom, we stood together at the counter of the fast-food restaurant looking up at the menu. A young black woman in uniform stood with a vacant stare on the other side of the counter. She was fifty pounds overweight and had a bit of food on the edge of her mouth. It looked like hashbrown.

A very large, bald white man on a cell phone pushed his way through the glass door. Behind him was a disheveled young woman and a little girl, maybe two years old. They stood next to us also looking up at the menu. On the side of the man's neck was a tattooed message: RESPECT GOD, FUCK THE REST.

The man continued to talk loudly on the phone as though we didn't exist. He wore an oversized football jersey, number eighty-six, and smelled like cigarettes.

"I don't know where the asshole lives," he said.

The woman lifted the child in her arms. She couldn't be more than nineteen years old, and somewhere underneath there was still a reminder she had once been attractive, before the drugs, before the backhands across the face, before the two abortions, the birth of her child, the three packs of cigarettes a day. She looked at me with a hatred I haven't often seen, her brown hair tied haphazard in a ponytail.

The vacant black girl wandered from her station and disappeared in back. A voice from the drive-thru intercom blasted, "Hello! Is anyone there?"

Bryan observed it all. He watched the large man standing next to him. The baggy blue jeans hanging down his backside. Tattoos covering his heavy arms. Yelling into his cell phone, "I don't give a shit what the nigger says."

The black girl returned to the counter, long beyond offended by anything whatsoever. She was chewing something chewy and staring beyond us, her body churning with cholesterol.

The intercom blared, "Are you open? Hello! Wake up, retards."

The big white man finished his conversation and put the phone away in his pocket. He squinted up at the menu, struggling to read the words.

Bryan said to the man, "One of the most glorious moments of my life was when my daughter learned to read. Watching her figure out the sounds of letters, and how they fit together, and seeing the world of words open up to her."

The man looked down at us with disdain, and then squinted back up at the menu, barely aware of his child and the mother of his child standing slightly behind him.

Bryan continued, "It's just disturbing to think that this pretty little girl will start learning to read soon, and when she begins putting the sounds of letters together, one of the first words she'll read out loud is the word 'Fuck' on her father's neck."

The man offhandedly said, "Screw you, Grandpa." He glanced up at me and added, "Fags."

I was extremely uncomfortable. I looked around the room for support, but there was no one. I felt naked again, and actually glanced down at my crotch to make sure I was covered. The black girl raised her stubby finger to her lips and pushed the piece of hashbrown to her tongue. Her face showed nothing while she tasted the morsel.

I wished it would end, but Bryan said, "I'm also curious about something else. What makes you think anyone wants to hear your phone conversation or your crude ringtone?"

At the exact moment he said "ringtone," the big man's phone went off in his pocket, extraordinarily loud, with a rap song repeating the word "bitch" five or six times in a row. He answered the phone loudly, "What?"

I whispered to Bryan, "Let's go. We can get something to eat later."

I expected resistance. I almost expected him to karate chop the big man and demand an apology like in the movies, but he just turned and we walked out of Burger King together. On the way to the car, I wondered if the whole world was like the inside of the Burger King restaurant and I'd just ignored it before.

Safe in the car, back on the interstate, Bryan said, "It's all about instant gratification. Surgery instead of daily exercise. Lottery tickets and get-rich schemes instead of education and working hard every day until you earn the money and respect.

"We want a magic pill for everything. Depressed, take a pill. Anxious, take a pill. Can't sleep, pill. Sleep too much, pill. We've got pills for people who overeat, for God's sake.

"There's no vision. It's the mentality of a teenager. They can't see past Saturday night."

We were quiet for a while before Bryan said, "Those people in the Burger King won't be invited to Alaska."

"What about the child?" I asked.

"She's savable, but realistically, she'll be left behind."

"Isn't that cruel?" I asked.

"Cruel?" he repeated. "Is it cruel when wolves kill the slowest buffalo in the herd? When they use the meat from that buffalo to feed their young to survive the winter?

"Is it cruel when the wolf starves to death because there aren't any slow buffalo left? How do we negotiate the terms of our own enslavement, Aaron?"

I had something I wanted to ask, but Bryan's last question pushed me sideways. He had the uncanny ability to rant endlessly and make it seem important. I thought a moment and said, "The book says people won't be excluded based on things we don't choose for ourselves, like race, sex, age, who our parents are, where we were born. But on the other hand, people are excluded based on laziness, propensity to drug and alcohol addictions, mental illness, lack of intelligence, or immorality.

"Maybe people don't choose some of these characteristics either. Maybe God chooses these. How do you reconcile that?" I asked.

Bryan answered, "Does the wolf reconcile her survival, or does she simply do what needs to be done for her babies?"

He added, "Good is good, bad is bad. Strong is strong, and weak is weak. All the civility, misplaced religion, and government programs in the world can't change reality. Whether it's God's fault, or the fault of the individual, some of us were meant to survive, and some of us weren't."

"What about atheists?" I asked.

"What about them?"

"Are they allowed to go?"

"Some people choose to believe only in themselves. It doesn't change anything. Do you think the guy in Burger King is an atheist? He hasn't thought about it enough to know what he is. So no, atheists aren't excluded."

Up ahead in our lane was a blue Mercedes. We approached from behind until the blue car was less than one hundred feet in front. A white fast-food bag was thrown from the open passenger window. It exploded on the pavement of the emergency lane, a cup of ice and a half-eaten hamburger flying through the air.

Bryan said, "What type of mentality does it take to do that?"

"Not a very considerate one," I said.

"Exactly. They have no consideration for anything outside themselves. No consideration for the lessons of the past, or fellow humans in the present, or the future of the Earth. The person in the passenger seat of the blue Mercedes is defined by his actions, just as we will be."

"Is Mr. Matson part of your group?" I asked casually.

Bryan smiled for the first time since we'd left Burger King.

"Until you make a commitment, Aaron, you won't know who's with us and who isn't."

"If a person wanted to make such a commitment, how would they do it? Is there some sort of contract to sign?"

"No. No contract to sign."

We drove all day and into the night, stopping only three or four times. I had a general idea where we were going, but we traveled roads I'd never traveled before and ended up on a long, deserted roadway.

It was nearly midnight when we turned down a dirt driveway and arrived in front of a cabin. There were lights on inside and another car out front.

"We'll spend the night here," Bryan said.

I felt hesitation. I felt doubt. I wasn't sure where I was or what would happen next. There was a sense of danger, like we were coconspirators, and any minute soldiers with rifles would pour from the woods and take us into custody with no consideration for the fact I hadn't officially made a commitment to the conspiracy. I'd yell, "I haven't made a commitment to the conspiracy," but they wouldn't listen.

My options were limited, so I faked confidence. The cabin door was locked. Bryan opened it with a key on his keychain. It was warm and comfortable inside. No one was present. There was no television or fancy amenities. A fire burned down red in the fireplace. Above the mantel was a portrait of a young, thin black man wearing a big white chef's hat. There were three closed doors leading from the main room.

Bryan said, "Your room is on the far right. I'm in the middle. Don't go into the room to the left."

"Why not?" I asked without thinking.

"Because it's occupied."

I saw a copy of *The Survival Manifesto* on the wooden table next to the couch.

"Oh," Bryan said, "and don't use your cell from here. You can call home tomorrow."

It seemed an odd request.

"Is this some type of safe house?" I asked.

Bryan smiled once more.

"Safe from what?" he said. "We're not doing anything wrong. This is America, right? It's not against the law to plan to leave. Not yet."

There was a noise from the left bedroom, like the sound of a spoon on glass. I glanced at the door. And then there was a second sound, the unmistakable sound of someone farting. I tried to imagine the possible connection between these sounds.

"Goodnight," Bryan said, and disappeared behind the middle door.

"Goodnight," I whispered, and stayed awake most of the night, compulsively writing notes about the events of the day and listening for brave new sounds.

I must have fallen asleep because I awoke to the smell of bacon. I could almost taste it in the air. After dressing and packing my bag, I stood at the crack of my door and opened slowly until the crack was sufficiently wide to see the kitchen.

There was a woman, small and Asian, moving from the stove to the refrigerator and back. She was neatly dressed, and from where I stood appeared to be in her mid-fifties.

Maybe she was the hired help. Maybe she was the future President of the New World. Maybe she was the origin of the two sounds made from the left-side bedroom the night before.

I decided not to wait until Bryan entered the frame. The only thing I knew for sure was this Asian woman was the first person I'd met so far besides Bryan who might tell me anything I wanted to know. The only person who could verify anything Bryan said. I made sure to close the door behind me loud enough to announce my arrival but the woman didn't turn. She stood in front of the crackling bacon pushing the meat around the pan with a fork, leaving me standing awkwardly ten feet behind her.

"Would you like some breakfast?" she asked.

Her English was pristine, but I still had no clues to her purpose in the cabin. Bryan's door was closed, and I could see his car parked where we'd left it.

"Yes, thank you," I said, and sat down in one of the four chairs at the heavy wooden table.

Over the course of a few minutes, the Asian woman brought me coffee, bacon, two fried eggs, and a biscuit. Her movements were smooth and simple, more than just a result of comfort, but a basic confidence. Without introduction or words, I could feel a presence of superiority. She wasn't the hired help, but she could cook a hell of a breakfast anyway.

"Do you know who I am?" I asked.

"Yes," she said. "Would you like cream and sugar?"

"No, thank you."

The middle door behind me opened. The lady looked over my shoulder, and I waited.

Bryan's voice said, "I see you two have met."

"Not really," I said.

"Well, Aaron, this is Lei. Lei, this is Aaron. We'll be flying together today."

Bryan sat down at the table with me. He said, "Lei is a member of the Committee you read about in the book."

I watched her pour Bryan a cup of coffee.

"It's nice to meet my first Committee member."

Lei cut her eyes at Bryan, and he returned the glance.

"Well," he said, "maybe not your first, I'm also a member of the Committee, and by the way, this is royal treatment. You can see how seriously we feel about who will document this event."

I took a sip of my coffee.

"Is your real name Bryan?" I asked.

"The Committee members don't use their real names. It's unimportant."

"But you know my real name, and where I live, and even how to get in my house when I'm in the shower."

Lei set a plate of food in front of Bryan.

"We alternate cooking when we're here," he said. "It was Lei's turn. If it was my day, we'd be eating instant grits."

"You didn't answer my question," I said.

"You didn't ask a question," Bryan said.

Lei spoke. The rhythm of her voice was almost lyrical. "You are a fine writer, Mr. Jennings. I have read everything you have ever published. You have a strong analytical mind and a gift of communication. The perspective of our history has been at the mercy of our writers. Books are the bridge across generations. If you choose to join us, your job will perhaps be the most important of all."

Bryan put a pill in his mouth and washed it down. I watched him patiently pour honey over a biscuit.

He said, "Did you know honey is the only food that doesn't spoil? They found cups of honey in Egyptian tombs, still edible, unspoiled, after hundreds, even thousands of years."

"I didn't know that."

"There will be lots of honey in Alaska," he added, almost speaking to himself.

"Who's the man in the painting over the fireplace wearing the chef's hat?" I asked.

He leaned back in his chair to look at the portrait like he'd never seen it before, and then bent over his food.

He took a huge bite of biscuit, nearly stuffing the entire biscuit inside his open mouth, like a child might do. He chewed and chewed with white clumps falling past his lips to the plate of eggs and bacon. A grotesque display, and completely out of character.

"You must really like honey," I said.

Bryan shot me a glance like I was a smartass, and maybe he was right, but nonetheless it made me feel uncomfortable again and reminded me I was alone with two strangers in a secret log cabin in the mountains on the way to Alaska, totally out of control.

I took a shower and packed my bag again. The night before I'd plugged in my phone to charge, but now it was dead. The outlet was working when I first made the connection, but during the night it must have shorted out.

In the main room, I asked Lei, "Can I use the phone to call home?"

"There's no phone here," she said.

"Can I borrow your cell phone?"

"We don't carry cell phones."

"Why not?" I asked. "Everybody carries cell phones."

"Why?" she asked.

"So people can talk to people," I answered.

She smiled. "The world economy is based on ever-increasing consumption. We must have more and more. Somewhere along the line phone companies convinced everyone it's better to communicate constantly with people outside our presence instead of talking to who we're with, or even simply thinking quietly to ourselves.

"But it isn't better. It's inconsiderate. It's mind-numbing. Text messages. E-mails. Calls in the middle of actual conversations, in the middle of lunch. Phones beeping while we sleep, while we make love, interrupting important trains of thought—it isn't better than it was before, just more complicated."

It wasn't so much the things she said, but the way she said those things. I felt almost hypnotized. Ready to throw my phone into the woods and think.

A car pulled up in front of the cabin and parked next to Bryan's. The two automobiles were identical, side by side.

A tall, skinny black man wearing a white chef's hat climbed out of the driver's side. It was the man in the portrait above the fireplace. He was maybe twenty-five years old and at least six and a half feet tall. Around the edges of the hat I could see his hair in cornrows.

I looked at the man, then looked at the portrait, and finally looked at Lei.

"That's the man from the portrait," I said.

She looked at the portrait and then out the window. There was a knock on the door.

Bryan came out of his room carrying his luggage.

"It's time to go," he said.

"The man at the door is the man from the portrait," I mentioned.

Bryan glanced up at the portrait and back at me. He offered no answer or explanation.

The man with the chef's hat loaded our bags in the trunk without discussion. He was workmanlike and efficient, except for the hat, and no one spoke as we drove away from the cabin down the deserted two-lane road.

"It smells like muffins in here," I finally said.

"It's the clean fuel," Bryan answered from the front seat.

"Clean fuel?"

"For the past fifty years our government and the oil companies have had the technology to mass produce clean-fuel vehicles. The reason they haven't done so is pure and simple: money.

"Do you have any idea how many countries, how many people around the world, how many families are dependent financially, directly or indirectly, on oil? All the engineers, oil rig workers, truck drivers who transport, automobile factory workers, gas stations, airline industry employees, motorcycles, lawnmowers, ships, tug boats, storage facilities, all the way down to the guys who make the oil barrels. Millions upon millions.

"A quick switch to clean fuels would cripple the world economy. Revolutions would start like fires around the globe. Forget about what it's done to our environment. Forget about what it's done to our health.

"Where we're going, only clean fuels will be used."

We rode in silence for maybe ten seconds.

The black man with the chef's hat said, "It smells like muffins in here because I had muffins for breakfast."

I noticed he checked the rearview mirror, and then checked again, looking past me out the back window. I turned my head around to see a car, again very much like our own car, a hundred yards behind.

Bryan apparently had been watching the other car in the side mirror. He whispered to the driver, "Do we have a problem?"

The car behind us was getting closer.

"What's going on exactly?" I said.

No one answered. Lei was sitting next to me behind the passenger seat. She kept her eyes on the eyes of our driver, and I kept turning around to see the car gaining on us slowly. There were no other cars or houses in sight.

"How fast are you going?" Bryan asked our driver.

"Ninety," he said.

"Well, shit," Bryan said, and I saw him lean over and fish for something under his seat. I heard the unmistakable sound of a pistol cocked.

"What exactly is going on?" I asked.

I could feel our speed increase.

"How much farther to the airport?" Bryan asked.

"Three miles," the driver said.

Lei pulled a pistol from her purse. It was small and silver.

"Come on, now," I said. "Really. Will someone tell me what's happening?"

We reached a long, straight section of road. Our driver suddenly whipped the car off the right side of the road and slammed on the brakes. My face was thrown forward into the back of the front seat before I could lift my hands to block the blow.

I was seeing stars, as they say, white dots appearing and disappearing, when our driver exited the car and slammed the door shut. Out my window I could see him holding with both hands a black pistol pointed in the direction of the other car. To my right I could see Bryan and Lei, both out of the car, doors wide open. Lei had her arms across the trunk, the silver pistol firm in both hands, military style. I could only see Bryan from the chest down, facing me, his arms and shoulders out of sight above the roof of the car.

I turned around to see the other black car at a dead stop in the middle of the road maybe thirty yards behind. With the dots still coming and going like white Christmas lights, I tried to focus on the driver of the other car. The details of his face took shape, and I squinted to be sure of what I saw.

"Oh my God, it's Mr. Matson."

I heard Bryan's voice above the car say, "Who's Mr. Matson?"

I looked again, trying to be certain. The glare on the windshield blocked a portion of the man's chin.

"My neighbor. Mr. Matson. He works in his yard."

Bryan's face appeared. There was the realization I was in way over my head. I didn't have the slightest idea where I was. A man with a chef's hat was holding a gun out my window. The stars began to subside.

The car I believed to be driven by my neighbor inched backward. The driver's face melted out of focus, and I began to doubt myself.

"It couldn't possibly be Mr. Matson," I said.

The other car eventually turned and drove away in the direction we had come. One by one everyone entered the car. Bryan turned around in his seat to face me.

"Did you hit your head?" he asked.

"Yes," I uttered. "It couldn't possibly be Mr. Matson, could it?"

Bryan explained calmly, "I don't know Mr. Matson, but you just took a fairly serious blow to the head, Aaron, so we're gonna pretend none of this happened. Okay? Is that fair?"

He turned back around in his seat. Lei put her pistol in her purse.

"I want to go home," I said. I can't be sure I actually said the words out loud, because no one spoke in response.

The driver, his tall white hat touching the ceiling of the car, pulled back onto the road and sped forward toward an uncertain future.

No one spoke for the remainder of the ride to the airport. I considered the possibility I was actually home in bed having a strange dream. The car pulled through a gate onto a private airstrip and stopped next to a jet, impressive and new. The tall black man exited the car and started to unload our baggage from the trunk.

The three of us sat quietly, Bryan and Lei staring straight ahead like everything was perfectly normal.

"Is someone going to tell me what happened back there?" I asked.

Bryan turned his head around to face me and used his calm voice. "Changing the world is a dangerous undertaking, Aaron. We have to use precautions."

"Is that why you have a bodyguard?" I asked quickly.

Lei giggled. It was unexpected and childlike, almost something from *Alice in Wonderland.*

"What's funny? I'd like to know what's funny," I asked with a tone of righteous anger, like I deserved to be pissed off, and I deserved an explanation.

Lei answered, "Larry isn't a bodyguard. He's on the Committee. He wrote the *Manifesto*."

"Who the hell's Larry?" I shouted, frustrated beyond comprehension.

The black man stuck his head through the open driver's door. The chef's hat held firm horizontally, the man's face floating sideways two feet in front of me.

"I'm Larry," he said.

I was slow to grasp.

"You probably thought Lei was the cook, didn't you?" Larry said. "Asian, female, must be a housekeeper. Black man, young, cornrows, must be a bodyguard. Wait till you meet the Russian. You'll love his sour ass."

A car, just like our car except white, pulled up next to the jet. We watched the driver's door open. A fat man, maybe sixty-five, began to negotiate his extradition from the vehicle. He was sweaty, very Eastern European, with several chins and a greyish complexion.

"The Russian?" I asked.

"Ivan," Larry said, and went back to unloading the car.

The inside of the jet was clean and modern. Down the right side of the cabin were five single seats next to five windows. On the left were two double seats facing two more double seats with a card table in between. I stood for a moment and stared at the accommodations.

"Used to belong to Barry Manilow," Bryan said.

"Barry Manilow?" I repeated, and found myself searching the cabin for some sort of proof. A poster. Maybe a signed eight-by-ten in a wood frame.

"Not really," Bryan said without smiling.

"Why would you lie about that?" I asked. "I don't understand."

The big Russian said, "Why would anyone lie about anything? Let's get the hell out of here. It smells bad."

His English was very good, with just the slightest hint of a Russian accent, but I couldn't smell anything.

There was no one in the plane except the five of us. The airstrip was empty. I found a seat behind the fat man and in front of Lei. Bryan stood near the door.

"Are you the pilot?" I asked Bryan.

Before he could speak, Larry entered the plane.

"No," Bryan said. "The black man's the pilot."

Larry ducked his tall hat under the doorframe and disappeared into the cockpit.

I found myself staring out the window at the tree line a few hundred yards from the airstrip. Once again, I imagined camouflaged soldiers waiting for orders to storm the plane, arrest us all, and take each of us to small windowless cells in a jungle prison.

I would yell, "I never committed to the conspiracy," but who would believe me? I spent the night in a secret cabin with two Committee members. I was sitting in the car when guns were drawn. And now I found myself on a private jet behind Ivan the Russian.

When we were safely in the sky, Bryan called me to the table. I sat next to him facing the back of the plane, and across from us sat Lei and Ivan. Bryan began to shuffle a deck of cards.

"You play Crazy Eights?" he asked.

I needed some questions answered. "I want to know who was following us back there. Somehow you forgot to tell me anything about people with guns."

Ivan said, "You expected a revolution with no guns?"

"I don't know what I expected. A quiet trip to Alaska to see a city being built."

As he continued to shuffle, Bryan said, "And that you will see, my friend. You'll also get to meet all the Committee members and learn more about the plan. In the meantime, relax. Nobody got shot. Nobody fired a gun. If you started counting the stars in the sky right now, Aaron, how long would it take you to count them all? One, two, three... like that."

I actually thought about it. I stopped thinking about guns, airplanes, and make-believe soldiers and started thinking about how long it would take to count the stars. Every star in the sky. One by one, only taking breaks to sleep or go to the bathroom.

"Thirty thousand years," he said.

It was a depressing number. Large. Incomprehensible.

"We don't have thirty thousand years," Bryan said. "None of us has thirty thousand years, so let's talk about today. Let's talk about right now."

Bryan dealt the cards. Lei brought us drinks. Ivan asked, "Do you believe in Bigfoot?"

He was looking at his cards, so I wasn't sure to whom the question was directed.

"Are you talking to me?" I asked.

"Yeah, I'm talkin' to you," he said, still staring at his cards like his eyes wouldn't focus. Like he was trying to read tiny sentences, his skin ashen, big bushy eyebrows.

"I don't know," I said.

"Yes, you do," he insisted. "Everybody knows whether or not they believe in Bigfoot. In fact, it's one of the few things everybody knows for sure. Forty percent of Americans believe in Bigfoot."

In the far corner of the plane I saw a wicker birdcage.

"Is there a bird in that cage?" I asked.

"Yes," Ivan answered. "Now do you believe in Bigfoot or not?"

"Well," I explained, "there certainly are a lot of people who claim they've seen the damn thing running around in the woods."

Ivan lowered his cards face up where they could all be seen.

"That's not what I asked you," he said.

It seemed to be some sort of test. Would I glance at his cards? Did I believe in Bigfoot? Why would anyone keep a bird on a plane?

"No," I said. "I don't believe in Bigfoot."

The Crazy Eights game proceeded. My hand was strong, two eights and pair of low cards. I played with Brad at home almost every night, and my skills were sharp. I found myself wanting to win.

"Why not?" Ivan asked.

"Because they've never found a dead one," I said, feeling good about my answer.

Lei was a slow player, contemplating each move like we were playing chess. She deliberately placed a four of diamonds on the table.

Ivan looked over the top of his cards at me and said, "What if I told you they eat their dead? Would that change your mind?"

I looked over at Lei, but she was studying her remaining two cards.

"No," I said. "It wouldn't change my mind."

Bryan piped in. "Ivan grew up incredibly poor. He's self-educated and helps provide the Committee insight into the minds of people in poverty."

"What does that have to do with Bigfoot?" I asked.

"Nothing," Bryan said. "I win."

He put down his last card and turned his empty hands to me, palms out.

He said, "We tried to comprise the Committee of seven very different people. Men, women. Different racial and ethnic backgrounds, ages, religions, education."

Ivan said, "I'm the old, fat, poor, angry Russian who believes in Bigfoot."

Bryan said, "I'm the token white, American, heterosexual, Methodist male with lots of formal education, a wife, two kids, and a dog."

I looked at Lei. She politely said, "I'm the cook."

No one reacted.

"Really?" I finally asked.

"No," Bryan said. "Lei is our Asian, lesbian, genius female. But she can also cook, which is good."

The bird chirped. We hit a patch of turbulence. Larry's voice came over the intercom.

"Would somebody feed the bird?" he demanded through the static.

Bryan said, "Larry is our young, African-American, intellectual pilot. He didn't vote for you. Larry wanted to be the official writer himself, but he can't be the official writer and also serve on the Committee."

"How many votes did I get?" I asked.

"Four. Everything is decided by majority vote, like the Supreme Court, except we don't have to play politics like kissing a president's ass or making sure the Democrats or Republicans are happy. They're never happy anyway."

"When will I meet the other three members?" I asked.

Bryan said, "You'll meet Luke tomorrow, and then Abdul and Adrianna the next day."

Ivan said, "Luke is the rich English boy with bad skin."

Bryan smiled. I gathered Luke and Ivan weren't best friends.

Bryan said, "Luke is mid-thirties, English. He's an idealist. Abdul is our oldest member, seventy-five, Middle Eastern, a very spiritual and patient man. Maybe he's our conscience.

"And Adrianna. Young, full of life, Brazilian."

I noticed Lei glance at Bryan as he spoke of Adrianna. It was a quick glance, but had meaning nonetheless. I reminded myself to make a note later.

"What happens if a Committee member dies?" I asked.

"The other six select a replacement, someone cut from the same cloth as the deceased."

"Do you believe in UFOs?" Ivan asked.

Lei fed the bird.

I thought about it. "No," I said.

"Me neither," he responded.

"Why not?" I asked.

"Because they never found a dead alien," he answered.

"Maybe they eat their dead," I said, amusing myself with the answer.

Ivan leaned over the table. I could smell his rotten breath and oily skin. He smelled like beef stew, spicy and thick. His face became very hard and disturbed.

"Maybe," he said in a low voice, "when we get to Alaska, we'll cook you in a big gigantic oven and eat your tender ass-meat with a fork."

I was unsure how to react, so I stayed perfectly still. He slowly leaned back in his seat.

"Who's Mr. Matson?" Bryan asked.

I kept my eyes on the crazy Russian.

"My neighbor," I said.

"Why would your neighbor be in the car back there?" he asked.

"Why would you have a bird on a plane? Why would the pilot wear a chef's hat?" I replied.

Lei was non-confrontational. She stayed away from uncomfortable situations, coming and going as the conversation dictated. She fed the bird again, as deliberately as she played cards.

"It probably wasn't him," I said. "It happened fast, and I didn't get a real good look."

Ivan and Bryan caught eyes with each other and then looked back at me.

I said, "Maybe it was just some poor bastard driving down the road on the way to somewhere. Maybe you scared the crap out of some insurance salesman or stockbroker who wondered what the hell was going on."

"Maybe," Bryan said.

The three of us sat quietly for a time. The cards were scattered across the table.

I said, "I think I'll go back to my seat and take a little nap."

Lei sat back down with us at the table.

Bryan said, "I hope you didn't bring your robe."

He didn't smile, but I knew we were both remembering our conversation on the porch when I was left exposed between us for an ungodly length of time.

My seat lowered back into a comfortable position, and surprisingly I drifted to sleep thinking of Adrianna, brown-skinned and Brazilian.

I woke up to the bump of our plane landing. Out the window I could see nothing except endless white snow across an empty field.

"Where are we?" I asked to no one in particular, and no one in particular answered. "Is this Alaska?"

I heard Bryan's voice say, "No. We'll spend the night here and finish the trip in the morning."

"Why?" I asked, my eyes still heavy with daytime sleep.

"Because I said so," Bryan answered in a flat tone, leaving no room for discussion.

The five of us herded from the plane into a snow-covered white van with three rows of seats. The location was desolate, with only a runway and a small building a hundred yards from our plane. There were two cars parked outside the building, both black sedans like the ones we'd left behind.

I sat in the passenger seat. The cold burned my hands. Larry placed the wicker birdcage in my lap. There was a parakeet inside, pastel blue in color, inches from my face on the other side of the cage. The bird only had one leg, and he balanced on that one leg with his toes wrapped tightly around the wooden perch.

Larry started the van and drove past the small building.

"He only has one leg," I said.

Larry stayed focused on the icy road. He said, "Isn't it interesting you only notice what's missing. You could've said, 'The bird is a beautiful blue color,' or 'His eyes are tiny,' or 'What's his name?' But instead, in front of the bird, you point out his missing leg. What if he didn't even know he was missing a leg? What if he never saw another bird before and thought all birds only had one leg?"

I once held hope Larry would become a source of information, but he clearly didn't like me, and I decided it was due to what Bryan said. Larry was a writer and resented another writer being asked to tell the story he wanted to tell.

"What's your bird's name?" I asked.

"Andy," he said, "and it's not my bird."

"Whose bird is it?"

"Adrianna's."

The road we traveled was long, and cold, and empty. We certainly had to be somewhere in Canada, but I didn't have the slightest idea where.

"This would be a very unhappy place to live," I mentioned.

From the backseat Bryan said, "You'd be surprised. Worldwide studies have been done, across continents and cultures, to find the happiest, most content people in the world. Did you know America isn't among the top ten happiest countries in the world? We're not even in the top twenty."

"Who's the happiest?" I asked.

"Denmark. Cold as hell. Nowhere near the wealth we have."

"Why are they so much happier than us?"

Bryan explained as we rode along the deserted road. "America is a machine. Greed runs the machine. It's the reason, on average, that we live in the largest houses of any country in the history of the world, and have the most cars, and swimming pools, and televisions, and everything else that feeds our materialistic obsession. From the day we're born we're hammered incessantly, brainwashed into believing more is always better. More will make us happy. More will make us content.

"But it doesn't. In fact, quite the opposite. Greed may be the fuel that runs the machine, but ultimately we're less happy than people all over the world who have less than us. Less food, less clothing, less jewelry, less square footage of living space, less technology, less media, less everything."

I thought about what he was saying. From the back of the van, I heard the Russian begin to snore quietly.

"If there are more than twenty countries happier than America," I asked, "what's the common denominator of happiness?"

"Family," he said. "Friends. Children. Safety. A hard day's work."

I expected him to tie the conversation into Alaska, but he let it linger. Maybe it wasn't necessary anymore. Maybe we'd reached the point of implication.

Larry drove slowly and carefully on the icy roads. There was still no sign of civilization when the van slowed and turned onto a side road. Trees began to appear in the whiteness ahead until finally we stopped in front of a cabin nestled at the base of a hill. Smoke rose from the chimney, but there were no other vehicles around the cabin. A well-dressed man stepped out the front door and stood on the porch looking down at us from the top of the steps.

On the way into the cabin, the well-dressed man embraced Lei, and then Larry and Bryan, and finally the Russian. I stuck out my hand, but found myself also embraced firmly with a pat on the back. That was my introduction to Luke.

The cabin was larger than the one the night before. Larry and Luke carried the luggage inside. Instead of three doors off the main room, now there were five. In my head I counted people. Five bedrooms, six people.

The Committee members selected their rooms like they were pre-assigned. I was left standing by my bag.

Bryan leaned out of his bedroom doorway. "You'll be sleeping on the couch tonight, Aaron. Sorry. The accommodations will be better tomorrow, I promise. But we'll have a good meal and a drink by the fire."

I felt homesick. "Is there a phone here?" I asked.

"Nope," he said. "Tomorrow you can call home."

The big Russian occupied the kitchen. I took a seat in the main room across from the fireplace. Luke appeared anxious to sit near me, which was certainly something new. At a close distance I could see his skin was indeed pockmarked and bumpy around the cheeks and down to the chin. He seemed very excited about my presence.

"We're pleased to have you here, Mr. Jennings."

Lei handed me a glass of bourbon. It was apparently the Russian's turn to cook dinner, and loud noises came from the kitchen. The fire was robust and hot, sap crackling. Larry hung the birdcage from a metal pole not far from the front door. The pole was silver and curved, about four feet tall, designed for just this purpose. Above the fireplace hung a picture of a gorgeous young woman, brown-skinned and Brazilian. Luke noticed me looking up at the portrait.

"Adrianna," he said. "You'll meet her tomorrow."

"She's beautiful," I said.

"Yes, she is."

"Why," I asked, "does Larry wear the big white hat?"

"I don't know," he said, and then asked, "Did the Russian say anything about me?"

"He said you were rich and English."

Luke blurted out, "I voted for you."

Bryan sat down. I watched him put a pill in his mouth and wash it down with scotch and water.

"I'm looking forward to a fine Russian winter meal, and maybe even a little vodka," he said.

After my second drink, I began to feel a little lightheaded and loose. We sat around the big circular table as Ivan served heaping bowls of borscht and some type of Russian sausage. I took a moment to survey the situation.

To my left was Luke, who hadn't strayed from my side since I arrived. To the left of Luke was Larry, perhaps the tallest hat-wearing genius in the history of the world. Next to Larry was Lei, small, quiet, and full of oriental mystery. Bryan was directly to my right, with a lively turquoise sweater and a fresh scotch and water. The large Russian squeezed into his chair between Lei and Bryan. He poured six shots of vodka, and while he poured I could hear the man breathing hard through his nose.

We lifted our glasses to the center of the table. After a moment of quiet hesitation, Bryan said, "Alaska."

Everyone except me repeated, "Alaska," and then turned up their shot glasses, setting them back down empty on the wooden table.

Only Luke made a face at the hot vodka sliding down his throat. The Russian seemed to enjoy his discomfort.

The conversation was spirited. Somewhere in the middle Bryan said, "Luke is an optimist. Ivan is a pessimist. But the world, as we all know, belongs to the realist."

When Ivan went to the bathroom, Luke whispered to me, loud enough for the others to hear, "He believes in Bigfoot."

I said, "That doesn't sound pessimistic to me."

"We all have our inconsistencies," Bryan pointed out. "We can only try to keep them to a minimum."

Larry said, "Because if we don't, then they're not really inconsistencies at all, are they?"

I had perhaps one drink too many and asked the question, "Do you really believe, truly, that you five, plus two other people named Abdul and Adrianna, can change the entire world, the course of history?"

The room became deathly quiet. The bird behind me made a small scratching sound with his one foot on the newspaper in the base of the cage.

No one spoke. From left to right the faces were hard and resolute.

The Russian stood from his chair, full of borscht and sausage. He leaned over and carefully filled each shot glass in front of each person at the table. When he finished he sat down and raised his glass. The other four Committee members raised their glasses to his, and the glasses touched.

Ivan said, "Yes, we do believe we can change the world. If not us, then who?"

They drank down the hot vodka, and Lei began to clear the table. Within minutes everyone had retired to their rooms, leaving me under a blanket on the couch. My head swam, and I listened to the noises from the bedrooms.

Something electronic, a computer or cell phone. A beep, followed by three quick beeps. Silence again. Running water. The tink of a spoon on glass, and again, the unmistakable sound of someone passing gas.

I had to urinate. I roamed around the main room in the semidark with only the light from the dying fire and realized all the bathrooms were in the bedrooms, and there were no new sounds to indicate anyone was still awake.

Of all the bedrooms, I chose Luke's for obvious reasons. I turned the doorknob slowly. It was unlocked. There was a dim light inside, and I quietly opened the door far enough to peek into the room. On the other side of the bed, maybe thirty feet away, Luke stood with his back to me, completely naked. His arms were stretched together upward to the sky, the muscles of his back and buttocks tight and tense, engaged in some sort of exercise or ritual.

In his right hand he held a small, sharp knife. I was frozen in curiosity and fear of being detected.

His arms began to descend outward in a slow, concentric circle, until Luke's hands eventually stopped against his sides. I was still contemplating knocking lightly on the door and asking to use the toilet, but then the oddest thing occurred. With the sharp little knife in his right hand, Luke gently and intentionally cut his white buttock. The knife seemed to slice through the skin like butter, leaving a small incision and a thin line of bright red blood inching downward.

It was disturbing, and the sensation of watching this inexplicable act left my legs weak and limp. I closed the door as quietly as possible and tried not to fall down on my way to the safety of the couch.

Why? Why would a man cut his own buttocks?

All the strangeness did nothing to alleviate the pressure of my need to urinate. My only choice was outside, and I turned off the porch lights to at least achieve some degree of privacy.

It was cold. A biting, nasty cold, different from the cold at home. I stood on the steps and pissed in the snow, looking out into the woods. It was brighter than my nights at home, and not just from the moon, there was a glow, and it occurred to me I had no idea what time it was. I finished, shook, and turned to go inside. One step, two, and a sound behind me. Before I could turn there was something against the back of my neck. The barrel end of a pistol, cold and hard.

"Do you have any idea what you're doing with these people?" the voice said.

It was a man's voice, strong, but almost pleading. Faintly recognizable. He had hidden in the cold darkness, watched me urinate, whoever he was, and now held a pistol to the back of my neck, maybe prepared to kill me in this Godforsaken place so far from home.

"Do you have any idea?" he repeated.

"I think so," I answered.

His tone hardened. "You don't have any idea what you're in the middle of, what kind of people these are. Do you care about your wife and children? Do you? Do you care about Brad and Sara?"

There was a moment of quiet. My bare legs were becoming numb.

"How do you know the names of my children?"

"We know everything about you, Aaron Jennings. We know every place you've ever taken a shit."

"What would be the purpose of that?" I asked.

"Don't be a smartass. Write everything down. You'll be given an opportunity to help yourself before it's too late."

There was a sound like his boot slipping slightly on the icy step. The cold gun barrel disconnected from my neck, and I seized the opportunity to bust through the front door, losing my balance badly, knocking over the birdcage, and then falling to the floor, face first, the heaviness of my torso crushing the wicker cage underneath.

With no time to contemplate the damage, I scooted backward and slammed the door with my foot and then jumped upright to lock it. I put my back against the solid wood door, my chest heaving in and out, my head swirling in vodka and guns.

On the floor, in pieces, was the flattened birdcage. In the rubble, from the light of the fire, I could see the tiny body of the pastel-blue parakeet, his lone leg stretched into the air, lifeless.

"Oh, Jesus," I whispered, forgetting for a minute the man somewhere outside, waiting, knowing the names of my children, telling me to write about everything.

I got down on my knees and picked up the little bird in both hands. He was soft and still. Andy was dead, there was no doubt.

The door to Luke's bedroom opened. His head appeared, and we looked at each other while I held Adrianna's dead bird in my open hands. A few seconds passed. Eventually, his head disappeared and the door closed. We were left alone in separate rooms, each with a strange and extraordinary secret about the other, and me with a great deal to think about.

I can understand now how people panic and hide the body when something horrible happens. After Luke's door closed, alone in the room sitting amongst the ruins of the mutilated birdcage, my first instinct was to destroy the evidence. So that's what I did. Before I thought it through completely, before I faced Lei, or Ivan, or Larry wandering into the kitchen for a glass of water and seeing what I'd done, I burned the pieces of the cage in the fireplace along with the dead bird. As the fire touched the bird's body, I expected the flame to burn blue, pastel blue, the color of Adrianna's one-legged parakeet. But it didn't. It just roasted and crackled leaving a black lump.

I sat on the couch for hours staring into the fireplace and thinking about the man outside with the gun. Did I recognize his voice? Was he some government agent making clandestine contact, wanting my assistance like he'd hinted? Or was this one of Bryan's tricks, a test of my loyalty to the movement?

I could have explained the accident with the bird, but not after burning the body. Why would anyone burn the evidence if it was just a simple accident? On the other hand, if I admitted killing the bird, Adrianna would hate me from the start.

I didn't sleep all night. The disturbing image of Luke cutting his ass with a penknife entered my mind. I took notes. I wrote down ideas and thoughts the way I'd always done before starting a new book. But this time the notes were real. It wasn't just a fictional character in a fictional storyline. I was in a mountain cabin somewhere in between home and Alaska with five strangers. People lurked in the woods outside. A man cut his buttocks. I burned a bird. God only knew what would happen next.

Oddly, I heard myself whisper, "Everything happens for a reason."

The idea was comforting, but it didn't answer my questions. Should I tell Bryan about the man outside? If this was a test of loyalty, Bryan would expect me to tell him immediately. If the man was truly a secret agent, maybe I needed to leave my options open. When the soldiers finally rushed from the woods, I'd need to show the secret agent my notes. He'd know I'd never fully committed to the Alaska idea. I'd taken notes like he told me. For the time being, I decided not to tell, but my mind was groggy and slow.

Morning came. Luke was the first to emerge from his room. He was fully dressed in a dapper suit and tie. His hair was combed back, wet from the shower.

I was still in my position on the couch, staring into the fireplace. As the room brightened from the light outside, Adrianna's face in the portrait looked down upon me as if she knew what I had done. Her eyes seemed sympathetic to my plight.

"Good morning," Luke said from the kitchen.

His voice was different, his glance prolonged. The differences were microscopic, but Luke felt leverage in our relationship. It was obvious, in a vague way.

"Did you sleep well?" he asked in his British accent.

"Not really," I said. I felt compelled to mention his odd ritual. To level the playing field immediately. Wipe the grin off his pockmarked face.

Before I could speak, Bryan entered the room. He stood next to me and said, "Did you know America spends six times more money each year on the costs of incarcerating the immoral masses than we spend educating our children?"

"I didn't know that," I said.

"Can you believe it? For every million dollars we spend on teaching our children right from wrong, making sure they have good instructors, providing books and safe schools, we spend six million to feed thieves, liars, child pornographers, baby killers. Six million to provide them televisions, clean sheets, basketballs, socks."

A small flame rose from the ash and cinders in the fireplace and then subsided. I wondered if it could be the beak of the blue parakeet finally igniting. The last identifiable piece of evidence.

"Can you believe that?" Bryan asked, and then walked to the kitchen to pour himself a cup of coffee.

"Actually, no," I said. "I can't believe it."

"Well, it's true. In Alaska, it'll be the other way around. Incarceration costs will be virtually nonexistent. People will only be held until the Committee can vote, and then expelled across the border immediately to fend for themselves. Our children will have the best of everything we can provide. I don't mean they'll be spoiled with computers, video games, and handed everything for free. They'll be taught not only to survive, but to expand the human species beyond survival.

"How can any civilization expect to continue when they expend six times more resources on the past than on the future? Six times more resources on housing old failures instead of creating new successes?" he asked.

Once again, I was struck by the power of the man's arguments. They were so clear I was left with the notion I was blind for not noticing such things before.

Luke cooked breakfast as the other Committee members awoke and entered the main room. The tension was unbearable, waiting for someone to notice the missing birdcage. We ate poached eggs on a bed of spinach, Canadian bacon, and melted cheese on English muffins. Nobody mentioned the birdcage. I chewed silently.

"Where should I take a shower?" I asked after finishing my breakfast.

Luke said, "You can use my bathroom."

Another prolonged glance. Another inflection in the voice. But I couldn't retaliate.

All Luke's personal items were cleared from his bathroom. The only thing remaining was the small paper wrapper from a Band-Aid in the bottom of the wastebasket. I found myself wanting to collect the evidence to be used later, but standing in the shower I couldn't envision how it could possibly be used. There was no physical evidence to support either of our stories other than a small scar and a black lump.

Through the process of cleaning the cabin and packing bags, unbelievably there was still no mention of the birdcage. We piled into the white van for the ride to the airport, and I purposefully sat in the back so my presence in the front seat wouldn't remind Larry of our previous journey with the cage in my lap.

In the van, Bryan recounted an article in a newspaper.

"A twenty-year-old man was driving his car in Miami. His eighteen-month-old daughter, Allison, was in the backseat in her baby chair. A police officer was driving behind the man and apparently learned the man had a warrant for driving on a suspended license.

"The officer turned on his blue lights and siren to pull him over, but the man took off. There was a high-speed chase through the streets of Miami. The man gained some distance between himself and the officer, but he turned a corner too fast and flipped his car into a building.

"Guess what he did next?" Bryan asked.

Ivan, in a hoarse voice: "Ran."

"That's right," Bryan said. "He climbed out the window of his wrecked car and ran. He left his eighteen-month-old daughter strapped in the baby chair upside down in the broken glass.

"He ran so he wouldn't be arrested on a warrant for driving with a suspended license. Abandoned his child to save his own ass. How far removed is a human being from his natural instincts to abandon his child to save himself from a few days in jail?"

"A long way," Ivan mumbled.

"And you know what he said to the police when they caught him a few blocks later?"

"What?" I asked.

"He said, 'Everything happens for a reason.' That's what he said. That was his explanation for leaving the child in the broken glass."

We rode in silence down the long, snow-covered road.

Bryan asked himself, "What's that supposed to mean?"

"It means he won't be invited to Alaska," Larry said from the driver's seat.

"How do you measure the sharpness of a circle?" Bryan said quietly.

Ordinarily, I would've asked him what he meant, but I didn't want to stir the conversation. I just wanted to get on the plane without anyone noticing the missing bird, and miraculously, it happened.

The jet sped down the white runway and into the clear blue sky. Luke sat behind me. After the plane reached a cruising altitude, I felt something touch my hair and tumble into my lap. A piece of paper, folded into a small square. A note.

In blue ink, the note said, "Where's the bird?"

The Englishman's torment wouldn't end until he knew I'd seen his insane ritual. I pulled out my pen and wrote on the backside of his note, "Where's the Band-Aid?"

I folded the paper and dropped it over my head into the seat behind. I could hear the paper unfolded, and then silence. The playing field had been leveled. We had an uneasy, unspoken understanding of sorts. He wouldn't tell the Committee I'd killed and burned Adrianna's pet, and I wouldn't tell anyone he intentionally sliced his white ass with a penknife in the privacy of his room. It seemed fair under the circumstances.

I was exhausted and closed my eyes to sleep, not knowing the length of our flight or even the time of day. I heard the cork from a champagne bottle pop and bounce against the wall. Bryan poured six glasses of sparkling champagne and delivered one to each of us. Down the aisle I could see Larry in the cockpit awkwardly holding his glass in view for the toast.

Bryan said to me, "We have a tradition. Before we set down in the new city, we toast."

We raised our glasses. "To Alaska," they all said in unison, and we sipped the cool champagne.

I don't remember much after that. Whether there was something extra in the champagne or not, I'll never know, but within minutes I was asleep. Beyond just sleep—comatose.

I dreamed about Cindy Sheerer, the doctor's wife, and Rita Blanchard from the Neighborhood Wives' Club. The women were standing in the manicured front yards of their large suburban homes across the street from each other holding long, antique Civil War rifles. From where I stood in the dream, I could hear Rita Blanchard yell, "Eat shit."

Cindy screamed back, "Pick up the acorns, or die in your yard."

I'm not sure who shot first, but the first shot was followed closely by the second, and the women began feverishly reloading their guns, pouring black powder down the barrels, stuffing the metal ball down the hole.

I remember laughing in the driveway, until more shots were fired and Rita Blanchard dropped to her knees and screamed. Her yellow sundress was covered in blood. Rita's face showed utter shock. The bullet had entered just above her right breast and exited violently out the back.

In the dream there was silence.

Standing in her yard across the street, I heard Cindy say in a normal voice, "Sorry."

There was a hand on my shoulder. I opened my eyes to find Bryan standing above me. We'd already landed.

"Welcome to Alaska," he said.

ALASKA

A limousine awaited. I tried to maneuver myself to avoid sitting between Luke and Ivan, but somehow that's exactly where I ended up. It was uncomfortable for a multitude of reasons, one of which was the sour smell seeping from the old Russian.

Our driver had Mongolian features. He was pleasant and alert, perhaps selected for his invitation to Alaska for those very characteristics. He didn't seem nervous, and neither did my fellow passengers now that we were safe within the confines of the new city.

The place was abuzz with activity. Buildings under construction lined the highway. They were set back from the road and spread out. Someone had planned for the future. There was very little traffic, no factories belching smoke or graffiti-covered walls. No stray dogs or trash on the side of the road. Clean, efficient, cool and blue.

"What do you call this place?" I asked.

"Jamestown," Bryan said.

It made me smile, remembering Bryan sitting on my porch telling about the courage of the Pilgrims, forced to rely on blind faith in a new world because the old world was no longer an option.

"Jamestown, Alaska," I said to myself.

Larry said, "If you had to guess right now, Mr. Jennings, based on what you know about each of us so far, who would you think decided the Committee should be transported in limousines so the average laborer can notice our arrival? So we stand above the other citizens?"

I looked slowly around at each of the five faces, and each of the five faces looked back at me in silence. It was a trick question.

"Don't answer that question," Larry said.

"Why not?" I asked.

"Maybe it's a test of your loyalty," he said.

"How so?" I asked, and thought immediately of the man on the porch the night before.

He didn't answer. We just looked at each other.

"We know you killed the bird," Larry said.

I cut my eyes at Luke. He looked out the window at the landscape, expressionless.

"It was an accident."

Bryan said, "Was it an accident when you burned the bird in the fireplace?"

I felt like a kid in the principal's office. There was no easy answer to the question of why I burned the bird.

I blurted out, "Luke slices his ass."

I was instantly aware my statement made no sense to anyone except myself and the Englishman, but like the kid cornered in the principal's office, anything seemed better than nothing.

But it wasn't. Now the car was quiet, and everyone waited for an explanation. An explanation of not only why I burned a bird, but what in God's name I meant about Luke's ass.

"I tell you what," Bryan said, "maybe we could make up a story. Maybe the bird got loose, flew out the door, found freedom in the mountains."

Ivan said, "He only had one leg. He'd be dead in a day."

"It was a parakeet," I said. "Even if he had ten legs he wouldn't survive a day in the mountains."

"What do you propose we do?" Bryan asked.

Lei spoke, "I propose we tell Adrianna her bird, Andy, passed away and was cremated, which is environmentally friendly, and we held a funeral for Andy, with music and kind words. I see no point in telling her the details of the bird's violent death or the aftermath."

Her lyrical, sensible words filled the car.

"Shall we vote?" Bryan proposed.

Larry said, "How can you be sure the bird was dead, and you didn't roast him alive?"

Ivan said, "I want to know about the situation with Luke's ass."

It just didn't seem possible that these five people, or any five people for that matter, could figure out anything whatsoever, much less the creation of a completely new world.

Bryan repeated, his voice a bit more authoritative, "Shall we vote on whether to adopt Lei's story about the death of Andy?"

The members conceded with their silence.

"All in favor?"

It was unanimous, and I wanted to get out of the car very badly. The limousine pulled in front of a large square building, no frills but very strong and secure.

Bryan said, "This is the Hall of the Committee. We have living quarters in the back and a guestroom for you."

"Can I use the phone?" I asked.

"Absolutely. There's a phone in your room. I'll come get you at dinnertime, and tomorrow you will have the tour of the city."

The Mongolian led me to my room. It was more than adequate. Large and spacious, but without windows.

I sat down on the edge of the bed and dialed my home telephone number. It rang once, twice, and on the third ring a man's voice said, "Hello."

I was stunned for a moment.

"Who is this?" I said.

There was silence on the other end of the line.

"Who the hell is this?" I asked. "Mr. Matson?"

The line went dead. I slammed the phone down.

"Is this what it's like to go insane?" I said to myself. "Is this what it's like?"

I redialed the number carefully. It rang once, twice, and on the third ring Sara's voice said, "Hello."

"Sara. It's me, Daddy."

"Hello, Daddy."

"Is there a man over at the house?" I asked.

"What kinda man?"

I caught myself in the midst of delusion. "Never mind. Never mind."

"Where are you, Daddy?"

"I'm in Alaska."

"Momma says Alaska is for Eskimos and poor people."

"Can I talk to your mother?"

"Do you remember I told you about George, the dumb kid in my class?"

"Yes."

"Is he in Alaska?"

"I haven't seen him yet, but I just got here today."

"Momma thinks you're having an affair."

"How do you know that?" I asked.

"I heard her telling Mrs. Blanchard yesterday. Mrs. Blanchard said you weren't worth worrying about."

"Maybe somebody needs to shoot Mrs. Blanchard with a Civil War rifle."

"That's not a nice thing to say."

"No, I suppose it isn't. Can I talk to your mother?"

"She has a headache."

"Can I talk to her anyway?" I asked.

"No, and my show's on, Daddy. I need to go."

She hung up. The phone went dead.

Had I called the wrong number the first time, or was there a man in my bedroom? A man who picked up the phone on instinct and realized he'd made a mistake? My wife had the door locked using the excuse of another headache. My children were left unsupervised.

I took a long, deep breath.

There was a knock on the door. Light, just barely audible.

I opened the door. It was Adrianna. I recognized her face from the portrait above the fireplace in the second cabin, but the portrait did her no justice. I remember being instantly struck by her absolute beauty. It was a physical sensation on my body, beyond lust, almost a touching, but certainly a feeling I'd never felt before, and I was left with no choice except to wait for her to speak.

"My name is Adrianna. I wanted to introduce myself before dinner."

I just said the first thing that entered my mind. "I believe you might be the most gorgeous woman I've ever seen in my life."

Her face seemed flawless in the light from the hallway, and without thinking, I reached out my hand and touched the warm brown skin of her cheek with my fingertips. She didn't pull away. She didn't change her expression, and it slowly occurred to me that my actions were wholly inappropriate.

I lowered my hand. "I'm sorry. I don't usually do things like that."

She smiled. "I will see you at dinner," she said, and turned to walk away.

I watched her move down the hallway. She was barefooted, her black hair pulled into a ponytail, maybe late twenties. She walked with an ease and lightness, but also with purpose and direction, not looking back.

I showered and dressed, feeling a bit like a schoolboy with a crush on a cheerleader. Just a casual crush. I'd never cheated on my wife, and had no intention of ever doing so, despite her suspicions, but my lonely mind began to imagine what it might be like. Adrianna.

Promptly at 7:00 p.m. Bryan knocked on my door. On the way to the dining area we stopped at the massive room where the Committee made their decisions.

Bryan explained, "The seven Committee members sit in a large circle around the circumference of the room. That way, no Committee member sits in front of or behind another member. The chairs are spaced evenly around the center circle. The presenter of the proposal stands in the center circle, presenting the information. We ask questions and then vote."

I asked, "So who is the presenter of the proposals?"

"Different people, depending on the agenda."

"And if the presenter of the proposal has his own personal agenda," I said, "then the Committee only hears one side of the story."

Bryan smiled. Again I couldn't tell if he was amused by my ignorance or liked that I'd raised such a compelling issue.

"Do people in Jamestown have constitutional rights?" I asked.

"When the American Constitution was drafted in the 1700s, it was brilliant, based on the needs of the times. Constructed with the safeguards dictated by the abuses of governments, religions, and the wealthy throughout European history. But it's not the 1700s anymore. The world has changed. People have changed. Civilization has changed. We cannot allow ourselves to be constrained by the words of a document, no matter how brilliant, that simply does not apply to the present world. Could you and I draft a constitution today envisioning what the world would be like in the year 2300? Of course not. It would be silly to try. The greatest quality of the human animal is our ability to adapt."

We stood within the large circle in the middle of the room, surrounded by the seven pedestals. I noticed there was no seating for observers, for the general public to come and watch the proceedings.

"So in other words," I said, "this is a dictatorship."

Bryan smiled again. "Oh no, far from it. You will see."

As we walked together down the long hall toward the dining room, Bryan asked, "Is there anything you need to tell me?"

It was a dangerous question. Open-ended. Maybe nothing more than a fishing expedition. But was the man on the porch, as I suspected, a test of my loyalty? A test I'd failed? Or was Bryan interested in what I meant about Luke slicing his ass? Or had Adrianna already told him I touched her face in such a strange and inappropriate way? Or was my phone tapped? I answered as quickly as possible.

"No," I said.

The dining table was also round, no one sitting in front of or behind anyone else. There was no head of the table, everyone had an equal view.

I was introduced to the seventh and last Committee member, Abdul. He was very Middle Eastern, wearing a white turban. The man was short and elderly. We shook hands and he smiled politely, somehow leading me to believe Abdul wasn't a fan of my selection. I deduced my four votes came from Bryan, Lei, Luke, and Adrianna, with Luke probably already regretting his decision. I held a precarious majority.

The food was remarkable, and the service excellent. "Remember," Bryan said, "we have the best chefs, the best hospitality service the outside world has to offer. And they, in turn, have the most gracious customers, the best tippers, the best ingredients, the best working conditions."

I spent most of the evening trying not to look at Adrianna, who sat across the table from me. Her hair was down, and I was given the privilege of hearing her laugh, our eyes catching between sips of wine and lively conversation.

I was beginning to better understand the odd relation between the very different people surrounding me. There were undercurrents of tension, jealousy, and suspicion, but these people were connected, like a family, with a feeling of permanence, as if they'd long ago resigned themselves to the belief they would succeed or fail together.

At the end of the evening, we held our glasses toward the center of the table.

"To Jamestown," Lei said, and the rest of the voices, including my own, repeated, "To Jamestown."

Walking with Bryan back to my room it occurred to me Abdul hadn't spoken during the meal. What's more, he seemed to be asleep.

"Does Abdul speak English?" I asked.

"Perfectly," Bryan answered.

"I don't believe I heard him say anything during dinner."

We walked further down the long hallway. The walls were bare.

Bryan said, "Separately, each member of the Committee is eccentric, nearly crippled in our individual ways. But we were specifically selected as a vital part of the whole. Together, we're almost godlike."

We were both fairly drunk, our wine glasses having been filled as soon as they emptied. I couldn't remember how many I drank. Maybe five.

"Godlike?" I repeated.

"Did you know thirty percent of all children in America are raised by a single parent? One in three kids don't have a mother or a father to help guide them through the world."

He didn't seem to expect an answer, so I didn't give one.

"My mother died when I was five," he said. "She was a drug addict. I can barely remember her face. In fact, the only thing I remember doing together is folding a load of clothes one time."

I didn't want to do anything to interrupt his memory or embarrass the man. I concentrated on his words so they could be recounted exactly in my notes. If I was to write the story of Jamestown, Alaska, the private motivations of each person would be important.

"It's strange, isn't it?" he said, and looked at me. "I mean, of all the things I probably did with my mother, of all the places we went, words we spoke, my only real memory is the two of us sitting on the couch folding a load of warm clothes fresh from the dryer, and the smell, and her hands." He looked down the hall. "Mostly, I remember her hands," he said.

We reached my room. Bryan seemed to snap out of his memory.

"Tomorrow, you'll see the city," he said.

I took a long shower, exhausted from the day, and then sat down at the desk to write a few notes about Adrianna, silent Abdul, the Committee chamber, and Bryan's moment of weakness. I was beginning to envision a book divided into seven parts, maybe eight. A story of the lives of each Committee member, and then the combination of those lives, like the combination of ideas and cultures forming a new world. A world not possible until all the parts inosculated.

In the corner of my vision I saw something small and white slide under the crack beneath the door from the hallway. There was a shadow, and left behind was a piece of folded paper.

My buzz was still thick, inseparable from the exhaustion, and for a long time I just sat and looked at the piece of paper, my mind spinning circles with the possibilities.

Was it Adrianna's hand under the door? That was certainly the most interesting possibility.

Was it Larry proposing a truce? Or Abdul writing what he couldn't say? Maybe Luke had drafted a compromise.

There was nobody visible through the peephole in the door. I transported the note quietly back to the desk and opened it under the light.

WRITE EVERYTHING DOWN. YOUR TIME IS NEAR.

is what it said, all in capital letters. The paper had no lines or identifying marks.

I wished it was trivial. A note from Luke or Larry like I imagined. Or even Adrianna. An invitation to meet for a last glass of wine. Glass number six. Instead, I was assaulted by the possibility of a revolution within a revolution—a traitor, or perhaps a government agent nearly ready to arrest, ready to set loose the soldiers waiting in the woods on the outskirts of the new city. Above all, and perhaps the worst scenario, was the possibility Bryan was giving me one last chance to come clean to him. One last chance to pass the test of loyalty.

There was a knock on the door. Again, light, almost no knock at all.

Through the peephole I saw Adrianna. My heart tightened in my chest and then began pounding like a little machine. Just the sight of her face through the tiny peephole made me silly.

She'd come to see me. Maybe below my field of vision she held a bottle of California wine. Maybe, and how ridiculous it would be, but maybe I made her feel the same way she made me feel. Weak and young.

Slowly, I opened the door until it was about half open, and we faced each other with nothing in between. She was still barefooted, and beautiful, with her dark hair in a ponytail. I smiled and waited for her to say something. And so she said something.

"Do you know what happened to my bird?" she asked.

The entire world fell remarkably silent as I searched for the answer. I was aware of the need for the answer to come quickly, free of guilty hesitation, and so I said, within the flow of the conversation, but in full panic, "Luke killed it."

I watched as the tears welled up in those big, wonderful brown eyes. It was a sad thing to see, Adrianna cry, but I couldn't seem to speak or move a single muscle, watching her from my half-opened door.

"It was an accident," I finally said, but it didn't seem to help much. It didn't seem to help at all.

I stepped out into the hall and put my arms around her. She smelled fantastic. Not too much perfume. Clean hair, soft, and I just held her and she held me in the empty hallway somewhere in Alaska, and I thought of that one-legged bird lying dead in my open hands, his single leg pointed to the ceiling.

I rested my face on the top of her head, my nose selfishly breathing her into me, until I felt Adrianna tilt upward, our faces coming together, and she kissed me.

The first kiss was small, almost innocent, but slowly becoming a second kiss, not innocent at all, wet and full, her tongue gently touching my lip, her eyes closed.

It was wrong. I was married. But it didn't seem wrong. Michelle had never kissed me like that. I hadn't seen her naked in five years. And here I was, kissing a woman like Adrianna, and seriously considering pushing her to the floor and having sex on the carpet in the open hallway, blind to any repercussions. More than blind, out of control.

But as quickly as it started, it stopped.

She pulled away and walked down the hall, her bare feet silent on the same carpet I wished was under her naked back. Her perfect ass moving perfectly with every step until she turned the corner and disappeared from my sight.

I was left standing in my doorway with a full erection and the distinct feeling Adrianna was on her way to confront Luke, the ass-cutting Englishman.

Down the hall, at the far end, I heard a door open. Lei, in yellow pajamas, stepped out into the long hallway. We looked at each other for at least ten seconds until finally both of us, at the same time, turned to go back into our respective rooms.

Lying in bed, staring up at the beige ceiling, I counted thirteen reasons I was unable to fall asleep. They stood in a row, like thirteen belligerent sheep, refusing to jump the fence and be counted. Refusing to be held responsible.

I finally fell asleep, but with no windows and no clocks I had no idea how long I slept. It could've been two hours or two days, but less than a minute after I opened my eyes the Mongolian knocked on the door. Hard and brisk.

He drove me and Bryan around the city in the limousine, Bryan pointing things out as we crisscrossed the streets.

"We've selected architects who construct buildings and homes based on efficiency and human needs instead of building the same old inefficient designs over and over. Why would we emulate something popular hundreds of years ago if it doesn't suit our needs now and in the future?"

"What's that?" I asked, pointing at a construction area.

"Our schools will all be underground. They stay warmer in the winter and cooler in the summer, with solar panels covering the surface. Our children will be safer from hostile attacks, terrorists threats, possible environmental contamination, natural disasters, and we can maintain protective security."

He continued, "How many school shootings have to occur before we change things? How many maniacs do we allow to take children as hostages, or how many schools do we need to see blown to bits by tornados, or burned to the ground, before we protect our children above all."

I noticed we were traveling down Albert Einstein Boulevard. Bryan noticed me noticing.

"The streets are named after people worthy of having streets named after them. Thomas Jefferson, Pythagoras, Eleanor Roosevelt, William Craft."

"Who's William Craft?" I asked.

"He was a kid on my Little League baseball team. He played seven years of Little League ball, and all seven years he was the worst kid on the team, the worst kid in the league. But he loved baseball. He loved it. He loved talking about it, and watching games, and I think he even loved striking out.

"I never saw him hit a ball in seven years. Not once. Not even a foul tip, but that kid never gave up on what he loved."

"Where is he now?" I asked.

"I don't know. I heard he drowned," Bryan said, turning to look out the window.

"That's sad," I said.

"Not really," Bryan responded. "Nobody liked him. He was obnoxious."

"Then why did you name a street after him?" I asked.

"Because I wanted to," Bryan said, without looking at me.

The Mongolian turned on T.S. Eliot Avenue. We passed a row of neat townhomes, much like a street scene in San Francisco or New Orleans, and then turned on Wolfgang Mozart.

"The heart of the city is actually a park. There's room for growth in all directions. Ninety percent of our trash is recycled at the three recycling plants situated five miles from the center of the city."

The limousine turned left on Murasaki Shikibu Street. A large stone building, much like a courthouse, occupied the entire block.

"This is our processing location for new arrivals. When families accept invitations, we fly them in from all over the world. They bring very few possessions—only personal items, photographs, things like that.

"The first stop is this building. They're issued identifications, allowed to select where they wish to live, and also select a job available in their field of expertise."

I watched a tall, European-looking man exit the building. He stood next to a woman, presumably his wife, and she held the hand of a boy, maybe five years old, who looked like his father, only smaller.

The man took a deep, full breath of the cool, fresh air, and watched the limousine pass. He held up two fingers in the sign of peace. It seemed an odd thing to do.

I asked Bryan, "What if someone wants to leave?"

"If you're invited, and you haven't been expelled, you're free to come and go as you wish, but you're not allowed to bring back anything. No money, nothing. And before you can re-enter, the doctors have to give you a clean bill of health. No viruses, no diseases."

The tour continued down Willie Mays Way, Henri Toulouse-Lautrec Circle, and Frank Woolworth Boulevard. I was impressed by the order of the design, the obvious planning for the future, the neatness. I found myself searching the gutters for a piece of trash, a stray napkin, a beer can. The people I saw were hard at work. Friendly-looking, but mostly they seemed to be interested in their tasks.

We arrived back at the Committee Chamber, and I was told I had two hours to rest before observing the Committee in session, actually voting on the expulsion of someone who violated the rules. I looked forward to a good nap.

Unfortunately, there was another knock on the door. Not hard and brisk like the Mongolian. Not light like Adrianna. Somewhere in-between.

I could see Luke's bad skin through the peephole. His face was up close to the door and he looked nervous.

I opened the door. "Yes?" I said.

"May I speak with you a moment?" he asked in his English accent, dressed crisply as usual.

I really wished he would go away, but he seemed intent on telling me something, and I assumed it concerned Adrianna and her dead bird.

We stood in my room near the desk, and I let him say what he came to say.

"Hear me out," he whispered. "I've a proposal for you."

"Why are you whispering?"

He ignored my question and continued to whisper. "We can help each other," he said.

"How is that?" I asked, skeptical.

"In exchange for your cooperation, I will accept full responsibility for the bird you killed."

He could tell I was interested.

Luke continued, "I will take the blame, tell Adrianna I was the one who tripped and landed on the cage."

I waited, and then asked, "And what do you want in return?"

Luke leaned forward. "In return, you will keep the secret of what you may have witnessed in my room at the cabin."

I weighed the proposal.

"But that's not all," he said. "Also, you must agree to portray me in a favorable light in your book."

He had two goals, one short-term and one long-term, intertwined, but at the moment, perhaps both equally important. I thought of Adrianna the night before, crying at my door.

Luke said, "Fate is negotiable."

During moments of great compromise, for whatever reason, we are sometimes not allowed recognition, struck blind like a momentary seizure in our bloodless brains.

What could be the harm in such a bargain? I had never intended to portray Luke or anyone else in a light other than favorable. I would just be promising to do something I intended to do all along.

Luke extended his hand to seal our contract, and after hesitating the briefest of moments, I took the man's hand in mine, and my fate was indeed negotiated.

Although I'd visited the Committee Chamber the day before, I was struck again by its vastness. The Mongolian led me to a table in the inner circle.

The ceremony was almost religious. After I was seated, the Mongolian disappeared and returned with two men. The first was a very dark-skinned man, coal black, with short-cropped hair and a grey suit. There were four hardwood tables forming a semicircle, each with only one chair, and the dark-skinned man with the short-cropped hair sat to my right.

The second man was a stout, forty-year-old white fellow wearing work boots and a baseball cap. He sat down and looked around the room like it was the first time, the way a man might look around the immense interior of a European cathedral, his eyes struggling with the empty space.

We sat quietly, the Mongolian taking the chair to my left, and waited for something to happen. On the table in front of my chair someone had placed a yellow pad of paper and a blue ink pen, encouragement to record the events I would witness.

I began to imagine sitting at a table in the center of the Roman Coliseum. The man across from me would be led to my table by two elaborately dressed Roman guards. With his baseball cap set back on his head, the work boot–wearing man would look slowly across the sea of faces surrounding him. The sea of Roman faces. The chants of the crowd would begin. Low at first, and then building to a circular wave of sound.

The man leans forward across the table to me and says, "What do they want?"

I listen for a moment and say loudly, "I don't know."

A tiger appears behind him, orange and black, and before I can warn the man, the tiger is upon him, biting his head, knocking the baseball cap to the ground.

But in the real world, sitting somewhere in Alaska with three complete strangers in the inner semicircle of the Committee Chamber, a clock struck two and the seven members of the Committee climbed the little stairs to their pedestals situated in a circle, with no one ahead or behind anyone else. From left to right I saw Luke, Lei, Abdul, Bryan, Larry, Ivan, and Adrianna. Larry's big, white chef's hat was conspicuously missing from his neatly cornrowed head.

When everyone was situated, the black man with the grey suit stood and said in a very proper and refined voice, "Today the Committee will decide the case of Gary Jones. Mr. Jones, please rise."

The man with the baseball cap stood, quickly removing his cap like he'd forgotten it was there, the way people sometimes do after the first bars of the National Anthem at a baseball game.

The black man said, "Mr. Jones is forty-one years old. He's married with two children, Gary Jr., twelve, and Helen, nine. Mr. Jones came to Jamestown eighteen months ago. He chose to work as a carpenter, and last week tools from his job site began to disappear.

"When confronted, Mr. Jones denied knowledge of the missing tools. However, it was determined he traded the tools for a new washing machine. The tools and the washing machine have since been recovered."

Gary Jones listened to the black man speak, but his expression didn't change. I found it all fascinating, as fascinating as sitting in the Roman Coliseum with the stalking tiger, and I began taking notes furiously.

Larry's voice boomed against the walls. "Mr. Jones, do you have anything to say?"

It became uncomfortably quiet. I scanned the faces around me one by one, left to right, with Luke staring directly at me and Adrianna failing to meet my glance. We waited patiently for Gary Jones to speak.

"No," was all he said, in a voice devoid of accent or emotion.

"Very well," Larry said. "You can step out in the hall and we will inform you of our decision shortly."

The Mongolian led Mr. Jones from the room. I saw a door open as the two men left the Chamber. The door remained open, and I watched the silhouette of a man lean against the frame of the doorway, arms crossed. It wasn't the Mongolian or Gary Jones. The shape of the head looked like the shape of the head of Mr. Matson, my mysterious neighbor, the man I once believed drove the black sedan following us to the first airport.

I squinted my eyes and tilted my head to the side, focusing on the figure in the doorway. He was just far enough away to make his features impossible to distinguish, but close enough to cause me to believe if I concentrated a bit more, centralized just a second longer, I would see the man for who he was—know for sure if it was Mr. Matson, or someone else, maybe a person I'd never met.

Abdul uttered his first words. "We cannot build a foundation upon thieves."

Luke said, "I vote for expulsion."

On the far side of the room, Ivan was quick to respond, "You've never done without. You've never known the feeling of telling your wife why the people down the street have a new, fancy washing machine, but she can't have one. You sit in judgment of people you can't understand."

Adrianna was looking at me, I could feel the pressure on the side of my face. I resisted the urge to return her gaze. Instead, I turned to see Lei staring over my head directly at Adrianna. Her face was contorted in a way I hadn't seen before. Like it was agonizing for her to look at Adrianna, but beyond Lei's power of choice.

I remembered her down the long hallway after my kiss. Standing, small and alone, the two of us waiting for the other to move. It dawned on me. Bryan had described Lei as the Asian, lesbian, genius, female member of the Committee. She was in love with Adrianna. I could see it in her face as she stared across the room, lost in her private lesbian thoughts.

Luke spoke. "I should like to take this opportunity to publicly apologize to a member of the Committee. A few days ago, at the cabin, I woke in the night and went to the kitchen for a glass of water.

"It was dark, and fumbling through the room, I tripped and fell, knocking over the birdcage. My clumsiness caused the death of Andy, Adrianna's bird, and I must apologize for the results of this unfortunate event. Adrianna, I am truly sorry."

The other members of the Committee either knew the truth of the matter or certainly suspected. What happened to the plan of telling Adrianna the bird had escaped into the great wilderness? Now, as Luke apologized for something he didn't do, I'm quite sure Bryan, Larry, and the others, with the exception of Adrianna, wondered what deal had been struck in the recesses of the Committee Chamber. It was then I fully realized the depth of my compromise.

I'd sold history for the chance to have sex. I was not so far removed from Gary Jones, who traded his values to bring joy to his wife in the form of a new washing machine, probably secretly hoping to be rewarded with extra sexual possibilities. Further complicating the situation, I was married to a woman other than the woman I compromised to obtain, however fleeting, regardless of love.

The tension in the room rose to new heights, reminding me of the increasing noise from the Roman spectators in my daydream. Louder, louder, until the tiger ripped the man's head off his shoulders.

I turned to face Adrianna. She was sad, but managed to smile at me down below. A smile that said, "I trust you now. And maybe, now that I trust you, I will allow you to have sex with me if you wish, and for this opportunity, the history of the world will be altered for eternity."

I came nowhere near standing and delivering the truth, but I thought about it. It flew past my mind, and for some reason I found myself staring again at the silhouette of the man in the doorway, until Larry's voice broke the moment.

"Mr. Jennings, do you have anything you'd like to tell us?"

Did he want me to confess? Was my agreement with Luke secretly videotaped? Was Larry talking about the man in the doorway? Perhaps the man who approached me on the cabin porch?

Maybe I'd reached the final opportunity to prove my loyalty and honesty. The final chance to show the Committee I was worthy of writing perhaps the greatest book in the history of the world about the most significant social movement the planet had ever known. The end of the Age of Excess.

I waited for a sign. Any sign from anybody.

"No," was all I said.

It was the same word left hanging earlier in the room as Gary Jones was taken away. Gary Jones, father of two, hardworking husband, who stole a few hammers and told a few lies so his wife wouldn't feel less important than the woman down the street whose husband cared enough to buy her the first shiny new washing machine on the block. A front-end loader with a super-spin cycle.

"Shall we vote?" Abdul said.

"Yes," Bryan said, and I tried, from the single word spoken, to ascertain whether he was disappointed I hadn't confessed and cleansed my soul, or whether he was simply bored.

Larry said, "All in favor of the expulsion of Gary Jones and his family, raise your hand."

Starting from the left again, I looked around the room. Luke's hand was in the air, as was Lei's, and Abdul's, Bryan's and Larry's. Five votes for expulsion. The hands of Ivan and Adrianna rested. Two votes against expulsion.

"It is done," Luke answered, and it was a good thing Ivan's chair was so far away from the Englishman. The anger was nasty between the two.

Gary Jones was led back into the room. His baseball cap rested on the crown of his head again like I'd imagined in the daydream.

"Gary Jones," Bryan said.

"Yes," he answered, again without emotion.

"The Committee has voted for your expulsion. You and your family have twenty-four hours to leave."

I watched Mr. Jones closely as the verdict was delivered. Surprisingly, he seemed almost relieved. It was the only sign of anything, besides bewilderment, I'd garnered from his face during the entire episode.

I knew I had to talk to him before he left. Understand why he felt the way he seemed to feel. There was a world being built outside the walls of the Committee Chamber, and there were people building that world. People other than the seven sitting comfortably above us on their pedestals.

As the Mongolian stepped forward to lead him from the Chamber, Mr. Jones looked at me sitting ten feet away, the blue ink pen in my hand, its tip touching the paper, recording history as it happened. And Gary Jones, the accused liar and thief, the expelled father of two, winked at me.

The phone rang and rang and rang, with no answer and no machine. I called home again five minutes later. Sara answered on the first ring.

"Hello."

"Hello to you," I said.

"Daddy! Are you still in Alaska?"

"Yes, I am. Are you still in your pajamas?"

"No," she said. "Have you found George up there yet? He wasn't in school today. I told everyone he moved away to Alaska."

"No, but I expect to see him any minute. Can I talk to your mother?"

I could hear Sara begin to move through the house.

"I think she's outside. Yeah, I can see her out the window. She's across the street, talking to Mrs. Matson in the yard."

"Mrs. Matson?" I asked.

"Yeah."

"Is there anyone else with them? Is Mr. Matson outside in the yard?"

I could hear the front door open and close with a bang.

Sara said, "I don't know."

I heard Sara's voice, the phone obviously held away from her face as she screamed across the street, "Mama! Daddy wants to talk to Mr. Matson."

"No," I said. And yelled, "No," but then I could hear my wife in the background faintly asking, "What?"

Sara screamed again, her voice now farther from the phone, "Daddy wants to talk to Mr. Matson," and I pictured her in my mind standing on our front porch, hands cupped over her mouth, my wife and the neighbor lady straining to hear.

I was helpless, in a faraway hole, and yelled into the phone, "No, I don't want to talk to Mr. Matson, for God's sake."

And then the phone went dead again. Dial tone. I hadn't spoken to my wife in three days. Now she was left with the idea I wanted to talk to Mr. Matson, and instead of calling Mr. Matson directly, for some reason I'd called our home and asked my child to go get the man. My child who stood on the front porch screaming, her hands cupped around her little mouth, the phone on the welcome mat behind her.

I started to dial the number again, but changed my mind midway. I lay back on the bed in the quiet room. There was another dinner scheduled at the round table with the full Committee at seven o'clock. I only had two or three hours to relax.

Things had gotten complicated. I reviewed the events of the past days. The drive with Bryan to the first cabin. The plane ride to the second cabin. Meeting each member of the Committee. How I'd slowly worked myself into this predicament with Luke, the secret agent, the man outside on the porch, Adrianna, the note under the door.

I tried to remember where I'd put the note. It wasn't on the desk or in the trash can. I checked the pockets of all my pants. It wasn't on the floor behind the desk or under the bed.

There was a soft knock on the door, unmistakably Adrianna's.

When I opened the door, she pushed her way inside. I peeked around the doorframe down the long hallway to gauge the reason for her hurry, but the hallway was empty.

I turned to face Adrianna, and she rose up on the tiptoes of her bare feet to kiss me. I was overcome by a sense of good fortune. By her smell, her eyes, the seclusion of our room, the idea I was someone else, so far removed from promises and obligations. It just didn't seem wrong. It seemed like a dream, and the dream sped on ahead of my conscience and the train of second-guesses.

She pushed me down on my back to the bed. I lifted myself on my elbows to look at her, and Adrianna unbuttoned her blue jeans. It would happen, no longer just in my mind, but it would actually happen. All I had to do was let it continue.

She undressed slowly as if I wasn't in the room, occasionally glancing over my head at the wall behind me. She stood wearing only her white bra and panties, her brown skin creating a contrast of colors. Her black hair free and loose around her shoulders.

Adrianna glanced again past my head, and I remembered a large mirror centered on the wall behind me. I didn't need to look. She was unable to keep her eyes from her own body, just as I was physically unable to look away as the white bra and delicious panties landed on the floor, and Adrianna, perhaps the most beautiful woman I'd ever seen, stood before me in the daylight completely naked and unashamed.

She slowly undressed me where I lay, and climbed on top of me. Her skin warm against my skin. We kissed elegantly, eyes closed, like the two of us were on a beach in the evening sunset, feeling the warmth on our faces, hearing the waves break evenly across the pale sand.

She reached back and guided me inside her. It had been so long I'd forgotten how wonderful it felt, and for the moment it was completely right in every way. More than just physically, more than just a perfect fit, but emotionally, spiritually, like all the pieces of me were together at last. Together underneath the gorgeous naked body of

Adrianna, safe and serene, her breath hot on my neck, our bodies moving together.

Afterward, I just lay in the same spot listening to Adrianna move around the room, knowing she watched herself get dressed in the mirror above me, her eyes never once drifting to my body motionless on the bed.

She kissed me on the cheek and said, "I'll see you at dinner," and then left me alone. I didn't want to move.

The phone rang. I bolted up.

"Hello."

No voice responded.

"Hello," I said again, and found myself scanning the room along the molding where the walls touched the ceiling looking for the lens of a tiny camera.

Still the line was silent.

Was it Lei? Had she seen Adrianna leave my room?

Was it Michelle returning my call? Maybe sensing my infidelity like a female lion waking from an afternoon nap in the Serengeti, instinctively knowing that her mate, a thousand yards away, is in the process of dismounting a new lioness, leaving both partners satisfied and content in the shade of a lonely tree.

I hung up the phone and took a shower.

As before, I walked to dinner with Bryan. Abdul's chair was empty. He arrived late and spent several minutes yawning.

Adrianna's face had a wicked little smile. I wished she would hide her happiness a bit better because Lei seemed to read the situation like it was written out in nice, crisp letters. She watched us both like a Siamese cat, quiet and slightly cross-eyed.

Luke looked pleased with himself. He laughed and talked, avoiding eye contact with me, focusing primarily on his Russian adversary.

Ivan smelled a rat, I'm sure. He knew the truth about the bird, having been present in the limousine when I made my unfortunate confession. And now his nemesis, Luke, was smiling after a public admission to a crime he didn't commit. The situation was further confused by Adrianna's obvious joy such a short time after learning of her pet's final horrible moments.

"When will you be leaving us?" Larry asked, the chef's hat securely back on the top of his tall frame.

Bryan interjected, "He hasn't told us whether he'll be accepting the job."

Larry failed to hide his intentions. He clearly wanted me gone.

"Can I ask you about the hat?" I said.

Nobody seemed to pay much attention to my question except Larry. There were two or three other small conversations taking place at the table, and as before, the food and drink were plentiful and good. I waited for his response.

He said sarcastically, "Can I ask you about the lipstick on your neck?"

No one appeared to hear what Larry said. No one turned and looked, stopped talking, or froze in mid-chew.

I thought of Adrianna's face buried in my neck. I reached up with my hand and rubbed where her mouth had been. Maybe Larry was the one who called my room and didn't speak. Maybe he wanted me gone even more than I thought.

The room became louder as the wine flowed. I decided not to drink much for strategic purposes. I needed to figure out a few things and avoid saying or doing anything particularly stupid.

In his big Russian voice, Ivan said to me, "Have you changed your mind about Bigfoot?"

When I didn't answer immediately, he continued, "Abdul here is a believer. At first he was like you, skeptical."

I asked Abdul, "What changed your mind?"

"Nothing," he said. "My mind changed on its own. One day I didn't believe, the next day I did. I dreamed of the Bigfoot. He was tall with a pungent smell."

I asked a strange question. "Will Bigfoot be invited to Jamestown?"

Ivan cocked his head and pondered. He seemed pleased with the idea.

"Yes," he said. "Bigfoot is honest and hardworking. Maybe he could take the place of the Englishman on the Committee."

Abdul was the first to leave. Then Lei, followed by Luke, Ivan, and Larry. Adrianna gave a look like I'd only scratched the surface. The floodgates of pleasure would open upon me as soon as we were able to sneak back to my room.

There was one problem: Bryan asked me to stay. It was less a request than a demand. He was intoxicated, borderline incoherent, more than just a result of too much wine. Adrianna excused herself and left me alone with Bryan.

He began explaining something. "Most of the time, I'm able to understand people's actions, behavior, by finding the connection between the behavior and our natural animal instincts. For the longest time I couldn't figure out why humans are so quick to take things for granted. Abundant food, a nice home, a loving spouse, all our blessings. I just couldn't figure out how taking things for granted was natural."

He kept his eyes squarely on mine. They were bloodshot, and every few seconds threatened to roll up in his head, but somehow the man was able to communicate intelligently.

"And then I figured it out," he said. "It's rooted in our survival instincts. Nothing can ever be good enough. No lair is ever satisfactory for the mother wolf if there's a better lair available. No food supply is enough if more food is available. Why? Because another animal will get it. It's competition. Survival. It's the reason our wives, the mothers of our children, always want a house bigger than we need. Always want more. It's the reason America has prospered. The entire country is based on greed. Pure, natural, God-given greed."

Bryan took a sip of wine. We were quiet. The waiters and waitresses were gone.

I asked, "Do you feel sorry for Gary Jones?"

Bryan focused on me again. "Who's Gary Jones?" he asked.

"The man you kicked out of Alaska today."

"No," he said. "Sympathy is for the brave, not for thieves and liars. If you're not strong enough for this, Aaron, you need to go home."

"What about the native Alaskans?" I asked.

"What about them?" Bryan said back at me.

"Will they be kicked off their own land?"

Spit flew from his mouth when he said, "It's not their land. Land belongs to whoever can take it, and hold it, and stay strong enough not to let another man get it. Like the wolf in the lair. No man is guaranteed anything in this fucked-up world. Not me, or you, or anybody else."

We sat silently for a few minutes. Bryan looked around the room at things unseen. His eyes moved from one area to the next until finally he rested his head on his folded arms on the table.

When Bryan's breathing became heavy, I snuck away, hurrying down the long hallway to my room in hopes Adrianna would be waiting at the door. But she wasn't.

I used the key to enter. Maybe she would be waiting in the bed. Maybe she had a key herself. But the bed was empty, and the room still, and I padlocked and chained the door behind me.

I lay on the bed thinking about all there was to think about. My time to decide was drawing near. My decision was multifaceted. What about my wife? Sara and Brad? My publishing contract? What about Adrianna, and the book of Jamestown? I expected to feel remorse, but the guilt hadn't had time to congeal. It would come, like a fog settling in a valley.

There was a light knock on the door. I smiled and stood from the bed, turning to look at myself in the same mirror where Adrianna looked at herself earlier in the afternoon. Checking my hair.

The view from the peephole was odd and distorted. I couldn't see the wallpaper of the hallway or anything familiar, just whiteness. The whiteness moved slightly, and then I was able to see the words written in blue ink, all capital letters:

WRITE EVERYTHING DOWN.

YOUR TIME IS NEAR.

It was the note. Someone was holding the note up to the peephole outside my door. How had they gotten it?

I struggled to unlock the door and remove the chain. I swung open the door, prepared to see almost anyone, but the hall was empty. At my feet lay the note, unfolded, with an extra word added:

TOMORROW.

I spent another long, sleepless night tossing around in my bed, listening for noises outside the door and thinking. I had one more day in Alaska, and according to the note, I would be approached again by the man on the porch or his friends. Whether they were truly government agents or Bryan's minions didn't much matter. Either way, I wanted to avoid placing myself in a situation where I was approachable at all. I wanted to make my decision of commitment without the complication.

As I expected, the fog of remorse for cheating on my wife settled around my body in the bed. I could blame her for leaving me emotionally and physically. I could justify the need on many levels, but it was still wrong. Making it happen, or even allowing it to happen was wrong, but now what? I'd tasted the sweetness of the apple. I'd seen how my life could be in this new world, with Adrianna waking up beside me every morning instead of a woman who didn't love me anymore, and maybe never loved me at all, never even tried to understand me, just spent my money, coveted others' possessions, played mediocre tennis while the kids were in school and the world burned.

Sara and Brad. Did they miss me at all? Did they wake up on the third day and say to themselves, "Something's different. I'm not sure what it is. Oh yeah, Daddy's gone."

How much do you sacrifice for your children? Everything? I lived in a house I hated, in a ridiculous neighborhood, for my wife and children. I wrote inane bestsellers so my family could have everything and more. I went to bed lonely and woke up lonely for the sake of keeping the unit intact. At what cost? Was all this temptation simply a test designed by God? Like a test of loyalty by Bryan, except on a larger scale, with eternal consequences?

I heard a noise in the hall. A scratching noise, like a small animal, maybe a hamster, scampering across cardboard. I listened, but the sound didn't come again, and I was left with my thoughts.

I needed to talk to Gary Jones. I needed to learn about this place, this fantasy town, from the perspective of a hardworking man on the street. A man expelled for stealing—knowing the consequences, but stealing anyway.

The knock of the Mongolian came upon my door. I removed the chain and turned the padlock to allow his entrance with a rolling breakfast cart complete with coffee, cinnamon rolls, a country omelet, and lots of honey.

We shared small talk, and I sensed an opportunity.

"Do you know why I'm here?" I asked.

"Yes."

"Then you know part of my job is to interview people."

His face revealed nothing. I didn't trust him to keep my secrets, but I didn't need to trust him, I just needed his help.

"Yes."

"I'd like to meet with Gary Jones, the man I watched face the Committee yesterday. I'd like to meet with him before he leaves."

The Mongolian didn't seem surprised by my request.

"If he hasn't left yet, I will make the arrangements and be back to get you in one half hour."

I peeked down the hall before locking the door behind him. If I stayed behind closed doors, or kept the Mongolian with me all day, I could never be approached. I vowed to spend the day either sealed away or in the company of witnesses.

Thirty minutes later on the dot, the Mongolian knocked on my door again. The peephole revealed he was alone, and I brought along my pen and pad of paper. We snaked through the hallways without seeing a soul and ended up at the limousine. It was a morbid, cloudy day, and we drove in silence through the streets of Jamestown.

The limousine stopped in front of a yellow shotgun house with a white tomcat sprawled across the front step. There were no cars parked outside or kids playing in the yard. In fact, there was nothing about the house that made me think anyone lived inside, except maybe the cat lazily eyeballing us as we made our way to the front door.

I rang the doorbell twice, and Gary Jones finally answered, looking much like he did the day before. He wore the same hat, pushed to the crown of his head, the bill at an upward angle. It seemed a silly way to wear a hat.

"Mr. Jones," I said.

Without anger he answered, "I already told the guy I'd be out by lunchtime."

"No," I said. "We're not here to make you leave. I'd just like to talk to you a few minutes."

"Talk about what?" he asked.

"I just have a few questions. I'm not with the Committee or anything. It's just for myself."

Gary Jones hesitated a moment and then swung open the door for me to enter. He turned and walked into the center of the house.

I told the Mongolian, "Will you wait for me here? I'll only be a few minutes. Don't let anyone else inside."

"Okay," he said, and I watched the man sit down on the top step next to the white tomcat. The cat looked at the Mongolian, and the Mongolian looked at the cat. They struck me as an interesting pair, and for some reason I wished I had a camera to capture the contrast.

Gary Jones was packing plates and silverware in a box. I sat down in the only chair at the kitchen table.

"Where are your wife and kids?"

"They left this morning," he said.

"Were they glad to go?" I asked.

"I think so. My wife used to tell me almost every day, 'Productivity is overrated.' Maybe she was right," he said.

I wrote on my pad of paper, PRODUCTIVITY IS OVERRATED.

"Why did you wink at me yesterday?" I asked.

Gary Jones continued to stack the plates in the bottom of the box.

"I think you already know the answer to that question," he said.

It wasn't the response I expected, and I found myself looking around the kitchen for one of those tiny cameras. The mood veered slightly.

"Why did you steal the tools and use the money to buy the washing machine?" I asked.

He answered calmly, "So you'd end up here, in my kitchen, alone with me."

The man finally turned away from what he was doing and our eyes met. He didn't care about the plates. They weren't even his plates.

"Oh, shit," I said to myself.

"Did you do what we told you to do?" he asked. "Did you take notes?"

Not only had I been approached, I had actually arranged it. I came to them, like they knew I would, and Bryan would learn one way or the other.

I asked, "Were you the man on the porch at the cabin?"

The face of Gary Jones had changed. It was no longer the face of the big, dumb, hardworking man on the street. It was different, hard like the face of a stone sculpture. He reached his hand out in my direction, a request for the pad of paper, my notes.

I ran. I bolted from the chair and ran down the hall. Wildly flying out the door, losing my balance, falling over the Mongolian and down the stairs. My face scraping hard against the pavement. The notepad under my arm like a football.

But there was no time for the pain or to touch my forehead for blood. I was up and climbing in the back of the limousine, the Mongolian scurrying to the driver's seat.

"Drive," I yelled. "Drive."

We pulled away from the curb with a squeal and ran smack over the white cat crossing the road, a thud followed by the second thud of the back tire crushing the corpse.

"Oh, God," I yelled. "Was that the cat?"

The Mongolian didn't answer. From my place in the back, I looked out the rear window. There was no one following us. The cat was lifeless in the road, a bloody white mess, nobody to eyeball.

I swung my head around. In the mirror I could see the Mongolian's face. He was crying. His entire face was squeezed in emotion, tears streaming down his cheeks. It was all crazy again. Gary Jones. The trap in the kitchen. The blood on my forehead. The dead cat in the road. And the driver, the Mongolian driver, crying like a child in the front seat.

"I'm sorry," I said, but he didn't answer.

A few minutes later the limousine pulled in front of Committee Chamber. I got out alone and watched the car drive away. I hurried up the steps and down the long hallway to my room, slamming the door behind me and locking every lock available.

I stayed in my room the entire day. No one knocked on the door and no one called. One minute I relished the privacy, the next I wallowed in the self-pity of being alone, wishing anyone would come to see me.

To some extent, late in the evening, I got my wish. Bryan appeared through the peephole and then pushed my dinner into the room on the same silver cart.

"I thought you might be hungry," he said. I was again unable to learn anything from his demeanor. Certainly he knew of the incident with Gary Jones. "What happened to your forehead?" he asked.

I felt the need to lie. "I fell down last night walking around in here in the dark, on the way to the bathroom."

It was a stupid lie, and I immediately regretted the decision, but it was too late to change in the middle. If he knew it was a lie, it didn't show.

Bryan sat down. He crossed his legs, reminding me so much of the first time he appeared on my porch not so long ago, a picture of composure with his neat sweater and fatherly look, hands together in his lap.

"Have you made your decision, Aaron?"

"No." I said. "I haven't."

Bryan showed a reassuring smile.

"That's understandable. It's a big decision. Tomorrow we'll fly you home. You can discuss everything with your wife and kids. Sleep on it a few days."

I liked the idea. It would be good to be away from this place. A chance to clear my head.

"That's a good idea," I said.

We sat quietly for a few moments. There was comfort in the quiet, the first comfort I'd felt from Bryan in days. I was hungry, but in no hurry to eat.

Bryan said, "You know, Aaron, eventually we're all trapped by the things we love."

I thought about what he'd said. I thought about how it applied to my life, and how it didn't seem fair, but fairness meant nothing to the Earth as it spun around and around on its imaginary axis. The Earth doesn't care about human concepts of fairness. It's too busy spinning.

Bryan waited patiently, but I didn't really have anything I wanted to say. So instead, he spoke again.

"This is what we'll do. We'll put you on the agenda for one week from today. You fly home, spend time with your family, and then come back. If you decide to accept the position, it can be announced to the open Committee on the agenda, and then we'll vote."

"Vote?" I said. "I thought the Committee already voted for me."

"We voted to offer you the job. If you make a commitment, we'll need to hold a confirmation vote. I think we can still get the four we need."

I started counting in my mind.

Bryan counted out loud. "You've got me, Luke, and Adrianna for sure. I think we can expect Larry, Abdul, and Ivan to vote against you again. That makes Lei the swing vote."

Knowing what I knew about Adrianna and Lei, it was difficult to believe Lei would support my relocation to Jamestown permanently.

Bryan seemed to read my mind. "Don't worry about Lei. I can keep her with us. You just figure out yourself. Decide what you want in this life, Aaron, what it means to you. And then just tell us yes or no. I'll take care of the rest."

He rose from his chair the way he had on my porch that morning. The morning I watched Bryan walk through my backyard, pausing by the trampoline on the worn spot in the grass. Standing where my children stood.

He stopped at the door. "Your driver will pick you up at five in the morning. I'll see you in a week."

When he left, I locked the door and ate like a starving man. The chicken was tough, and midway through the meal, I stopped. On the plate, just along the edge of what appeared to be a baked breast, I could see a small patch of white fur.

In the bathroom I shoved a finger down my throat, vomiting what looked like bits of chewed meat from the white tomcat.

CONTEMPLATION

I pushed the silver cart into the empty hallway and tried to go to sleep. Why would anyone feed me cat meat? Besides myself, only two other people were present for the unfortunate incident: Gary Jones (if that was his real name) and the Mongolian. Maybe it was my imagination running wild in a wild place. I looked forward to the opportunity to clear my head.

I was packed and ready when the Mongolian knocked on the door to take me to the airport. The anticipation of his arrival made me anxious. If he was the mastermind of my cat-meat dinner, would I know from the expression on his round face, or would we be like awkward ex-lovers with nothing to talk about?

I opened the door. He was very businesslike. A nod as he passed on the way to the luggage. I decided to apologize.

"I'm sorry about yesterday. It was a big mix-up."

The Mongolian turned his stout body around to face me. He looked as though he had something to say. Something important. But the moment passed, and I found myself following the man through the maze of hallways to the entrance where his car waited.

The idea had entered my mind to say goodbye to Adrianna, but I knew it would be a mistake. She would have come to me if she could. I suspected Adrianna was being watched closely.

I climbed aboard the same plane in which I'd arrived days before. I took the last seat in the single-seat row of five chairs against the windows. The Mongolian disappeared before I had the chance to say goodbye. He left me alone in the empty plane.

The world became very quiet, and honestly, I'd reached the point where I was painfully aware anything whatsoever was possible. Bigfoot himself might just enter the cockpit and fly us into the great blue sky.

I heard a noise behind me and turned slowly. In the back of the plane I could see a birdcage, much like the wooden cage I'd accidently crushed in the mountain cabin. I unbuckled my seatbelt and approached slowly. Inside the cage was another bird, another parakeet, but this one was gold. Gold like the color of a sunrise. When I got closer, the bird began to chirp.

I put my face up to the tiny bamboo bars of the cage. Unbelievably, just like Adrianna's bird, the golden parakeet had only one leg. He balanced with his toes wrapped tightly around the dowel. There was a nub where the second leg should be.

"What the hell?" I whispered to myself.

There was a loud noise from the front of the plane. The door swung open, and a man entered. Maybe seventy years old. Short. Five foot two or three at most, his body in proportion to his height.

The man wore a blue sport jacket and had a full head of grey hair. He sat down across the aisle from my seat at the card table. Not long afterward the plane began to move. I hadn't seen anyone enter the cockpit, but the door was closed.

We didn't speak. His chair was slightly in front of mine, and therefore I had the advantage of observation. He didn't turn around or even glance in my direction. After the period of discomfort passed, I found myself exhausted, fighting to keep my eyes open and eventually losing the fight.

I think the dream started immediately. Why is it when we dream we don't see the world from our own eyes, but instead, we see ourselves from a distance? A perspective which we can't possibly attain in reality.

In the dream I arrived in front of my family home at noon in a black limousine. I remember being disappointed no one was in the yard to greet me.

I carried my own bag, which for some reason had become a huge navy-blue duffle, up to the front door of the house. For effect, I rang the doorbell, hoping my children would race to the door to see their world-traveling father.

There was no answer. I rang again, and then a third time. I heard movement inside the house. The door opened. Mr. Matson stood in front of me. I turned to look over my shoulder at his house across the street making certain I hadn't gone to the wrong front door.

"What can I do for you?" he asked casually.

I heard Michelle's voice from the kitchen area. "Who is it, honey?"

"It's Aaron," he said.

Michelle came to the door and stood next to Mr. Matson.

"What's going on here?" I asked in the dream.

Michelle wore her tennis outfit. She looked younger, very clean and wholesome, with an obvious boob job. Her breasts were twice the size they'd been before, firm and full. I caught myself glancing at the cleavage.

She said, "We thought you were dead, Aaron. When a person is missing for seven years, the law presumes them dead. You couldn't expect me to be alone the rest of my life, the grieving widow. Could you?"

Sara walked past the door behind her mother. She was the same age she'd been when I left.

"It couldn't be seven years, Michelle. Sara's still only six," I said.

"She's small for her age," Michelle said. "Besides, I'm married to Carl now. The three most important things in life are a nice car, hair, and a new outfit."

I remember being surprised his first name was Carl.

"You married Mr. Matson?" I asked, but before she could answer, I woke up to the sound of crying.

Across the aisle from me, the small seventy-year-old man was crying. It was genuine. No rehearsed drama. No demand for attention. The little man was crying and couldn't stop himself.

"Are you okay?" I asked, but he didn't answer, and a few hours later, when we stopped at the airport near the mountain cabin, the little man left the plane while I was in the bathroom. I never saw him again, but he left something in my seat. A small black thing. The size of a silver dollar. I'd seen one before. It was a sea bean, dark and hard, with a smooth outer surface. They wash ashore all over the world, floating across oceans from faraway places. My grandfather used to tell me they were wishing beans, good for one wish. I hadn't touched a sea bean in years.

I spent the second leg of the trip thinking about my decision. I had a week to weigh my life. To go or not to go? To allow the inertia of my existence to keep me entrenched in the comfort of familiarity, or jump off the edge of my world with a pen in one hand and a wishing bean in the other to write the greatest story of my generation? Would my choice be dictated by the pangs of midlife, the weakness of ego, fear, obligation to family, Sara's next smile, Adrianna's naked body, or something else? Something I hadn't considered yet?

Would the answer come to me in a moment of clarity, or would I struggle until the last instant, undermined by indecision, at the mercy of the last crisp breeze? Swaying like a tall pine tree in one direction and then the other.

The plane shuddered. I felt the jolt of unsteady air. There was a flash of lightning out the window. I pulled my seatbelt tight and held the sea bean in the sweaty palm of my left hand.

For the next hour the airplane shook and bounced violently. At times the lights inside would sputter, go out completely, and then illuminate again. I closed my eyes and thought about dying. Thought about the plane crash, my body in the field, and the funeral. My breath would catch at the flash of lightning and I would exhale only after the thunder rolled away. I wondered who was in the cockpit, my life in their hands. Certainly not Bigfoot.

I held the wishing bean up to my lips, remembering my grandfather and the way he used to make his wishes, whispering to the bean just low enough so I couldn't hear the words. And then I used up my only wish in a whisper. Less than one hour later we landed at an airport not far from my hometown, safe and alive.

A car waited for me. It was just like Bryan's car, a black sedan. The driver introduced himself as Stacey. He was thin and girlish, making no effort to hide his feminine tendencies.

"What time is it?" I asked.

"Two twelve in the morning," he said. "I'll have you home by three thirty."

He talked the entire ride. I recounted to myself the events of the past days in Alaska. It seemed as distant and unreal as my crazy dream of Michelle's new breasts and Mr. Matson moving into my home. Somewhere along the line, the universe had spun out of control like a yo-yo off the string.

I was glad to pull up in front of my house. Glad to be away from Stacey's voice. From the porch I watched him drive out of the neighborhood. Across the street, Mr. Matson's house was dark. Not a single light inside or out. He usually left the porch light burning at night, so somehow it seemed extra dark without it.

I put the key in the lock of my front door. It wouldn't fit. I tried each of the other keys on the ring, like maybe I'd lost my mind and forgotten which key was the house key. The copper-colored square one. It was always the house key. Always had been. But now it didn't fit.

I thought I heard a noise from across the street. I stood upright silently and looked at the dark house. Nothing.

I went around the back of my house to try the other doors. I fumbled in the darkness, but the result was the same. The key didn't fit. I finally quit trying. It would be daybreak in a few hours. I laid out on the trampoline with my head on my bag, looking up at nothing. The stars were hidden behind a black blanket.

If Mr. Matson was out of town, maybe this was the chance to look around his house. No one knew I was even home. It was three thirty in the morning.

I stood by the side of my house in the dark shadows, looking across the street. Nothing. Stillness.

If I got caught, I'd have an acceptable excuse. My key didn't work. I thought maybe the Matsons still had our spare. It was good enough to keep me from getting arrested. Besides, if they weren't home, how would I get caught? Mr. Matson didn't have a dog.

I walked across the street at an even pace, no hurry, and up to the Matsons' front porch. There was nothing to see through the windows except the green numbers of a digital clock on the stove. I walked quietly around to the back and opened the wooden gate. The yard was always immaculate. Perfectly manicured bushes. Color-coordinated flowers. Big green hanging ferns. Almost too perfect.

The house on the right side had a floodlight in the back. I was able to see something in the middle of the Matsons' backyard. Something big, the size of a small car, and white, in the middle of the lush lawn.

I tilted my head to bring the object into focus, and moved slowly in its direction. Not until I was less than ten feet away was I able to distinguish the features.

It was an airplane. A small, compact car-sized, white airplane, with numbers painted on the tail and everything. A spy drone. Probably used to gather information, take photographs from above, and land at night in a confined space.

Behind me, inside the Matsons' house, a light turned on. Keeping my body remaining still, I turned my head slowly toward it. It was a lamp in the living room on a table by the aqua couch. I couldn't see anybody, just the furniture, and like I'd done in the home of Gary Jones, I bolted. Ran like hell through the open wooden gate and across the street, around the back of my house, and flew onto the trampoline like a teenager. I was breathing heavily. Maybe it was some type of timer lamp going off and on at strange hours to scare potential burglars. Maybe the Matsons were home after all, the car hidden in the garage, and they'd simply forgotten to turn on the porch light. One thing I was sure about, they had a damn airplane in their backyard, with numbers painted on the tail and everything.

Eventually, even with all the excitement, I fell asleep on the trampoline and awoke to Brad and Sara jumping all around me like two wacky monkeys. The first sound I heard was their laughter, and it was a good sound to hear.

The children treated me as if I'd never been gone, and I wondered if maybe their sense of time hadn't developed yet, the way a dog cannot distinguish between his owner being gone thirty minutes or two days. He's just happy his master returns.

Michelle also acted like I'd never been gone, for different reasons. I got a half-hearted kiss, cool and distant, but despite her aloofness, I found myself looking at Michelle's rear end as she walked out of the kitchen in a new tennis outfit. I could never tell her about Adrianna. There would be no way to have the conversation. No way to explain how lonely I felt crawling into bed each night with a woman I still desired who quite obviously did not desire me. Perhaps the only sadder thing would be the day in the future I'd feel nothing for her, and we'd pass each other in the house without a twitch of emotion from either side.

Even with all the complicated undercurrents, I felt comfortable in my home again. I sat at my desk in my robe with a cup of coffee, making notes about everything I could remember from the trip to Alaska. I changed my mind about separating the book into sections dedicated to each of the Committee members, and decided the movement, the foundation of ideas, the historical moment, was far more important than the individuals involved. The characters would all play a role, but if the book was to be considered timeless, studied for generations, Committee members would come and go, leaving the fundamental concepts to resonate forever.

I needed additional notepads and a fresh pen. Brad reluctantly agreed to go with me to my favorite office supply store on the other side of town. It was the only place that carried the pen that felt best in my hand, and sometimes I would buy three or four each visit because I held a baseless fear the company was on the verge of phasing out the particular pen I loved.

"How's everything been around the house while I was gone?" I asked on the drive, hoping to gather some information.

"Good," Brad said.

"Did somebody come over and change the locks?"

"No," he said, and began pointing each of the air-conditioning vents in his own direction, blowing his hair in the cold breeze.

"Did the Matsons stop by?" I asked.

"Who are the Matsons?" he asked.

Brad flipped down the visor and put his face very close to the mirror, examining the pores on his nose.

I pulled onto the interstate and watched him closely for any signs of avoiding my questions. I couldn't see any. He looked like a ten-year-old boy lost in his ten-year-old world, mercifully oblivious. Nobody had warned me he'd reach a point where he didn't want to hang around with me anymore.

We found ourselves behind two vehicles, a yellow car in the right lane and a green car in the left, traveling the same speed with faster-moving cars piling up behind.

The green car inched slightly forward but failed to pass or move over into the right lane.

"It never ceases to amaze me," I said to Brad as he examined his forehead, "how people are incapable of understanding the four-lane interstate system. The entire system is dependent upon drivers recognizing the fact that it only works if they move to the right, allowing faster cars to pass. This lady seems to have no awareness whatsoever she is the cause of all of this."

Brad seemed to find something new near his hairline.

"Maybe she doesn't care," he said.

"Maybe she's too stupid to care," I responded.

"Maybe we should kill her," Brad said.

I reflected a moment on his comment. He wasn't serious.

I said, "Instead of killing her, maybe we could just leave her behind and find a place to live where people are more considerate. What would you think about moving to a place like that?"

Brad tilted his head back and looked up his nose for a lengthy period of time.

"Why do people grow hair in their noses? It's a stupid place to grow hair," he commented.

The green car finally moved over and turned on its blinkers exiting at the same road where I intended to turn. We followed the car into the parking lot of the office supply store. The lot was crowded, and we were forced to park a distance from the door. As we were walking to the entrance, I saw the green car park directly in front of the store in a designated handicapped space.

There was no handicapped decal hanging from the rearview mirror. There was no handicapped symbol on the license plate. A perfectly healthy-looking, slightly plump, thirty-five-year-old woman exited the green car and walked into the store ahead of us.

"Can you believe that?" I said to Brad. "That woman parked in a handicapped spot. It's the same woman that held up everybody on the highway."

"Maybe that's why she was driving so slow," Brad said. "Because she's handicapped."

I felt my teeth grit. "She's not handicapped, son. She's just lazy and inconsiderate and stupid."

There were only two pens left. I grabbed them both and asked the droopy-eyed young man at the register, "Do you have any more of these pens?"

"No," he said. "They don't make those anymore. They're discontinued."

On the ledger sheet of my ultimate decision to go or not to go to Alaska, the discontinuation of my favorite pen would be a mark on the side of the ledger for leaving, in addition to the lady in the green car.

Later that evening, after the kids had gone to bed, I had a drink and caught myself peeking out the front window at the house across the street. It was completely dark again, with no cars in the driveway, and I wondered if the small airplane was where I'd found it the previous night.

Michelle shuffled into the kitchen in pajamas and slippers and began preparing her nightly protein smoothie, adding the ingredient du jour recommended by the latest magazine and totally guaranteed to reverse God's aging process, restoring a woman's dependence upon her beauty and velvet skin.

"Michelle, can we talk a minute?" I asked.

We sat down at the kitchen table. She sipped her smoothie. I sipped my whiskey.

"My key wouldn't open the door last night," I said, without accusation.

"There must be something wrong with your key. Mine still works."

Just like Brad, she didn't seem to be hiding anything, neck-deep in her life of modern materialism, primarily concerned with the excess skin hanging beneath her upper arms on the backhand follow-through.

In the middle of my second whiskey, I found myself disgusted by my wife. Maybe it was a psychological and physical reaction caused by my guilt over cheating, I don't know, but I wanted to scream, "It was your fault. You never touched me. There was no reassurance. What did you expect?"

Instead I said, "We've been invited to join a colony in Alaska. A new world. A place where only competent, hardworking people will live. They have a manifesto."

She took another sip of her smoothie. It was pinkish grey in color, and a thin line of liquid remained on Michelle's upper lip like a cartoon mustache.

"Hmmm," she said, which wasn't really a word.

"They've asked me to be the writer, kinda like a historian. Write a book about the movement. I've been to the city, Jamestown. It's an opportunity to be involved in something big, something important, God's plan."

She looked at me with a fixed expression, like she was thinking about something else, maybe the next day's grocery list, checking off each item in her mind. The cartoon mustache made Michelle look clown-like, and I began to see the features of her face like it was the first time we'd ever met—not just taking for granted the lines and details I'd seen a million times, but actually looking behind the memorization.

She said, "Since when have you been so spiritual?"

It occurred to me that we didn't know each other very well anymore. We'd reduced each other to stereotypes, two-dimensional photographs, exaggerated caricatures. I was too busy writing and providing. She was too busy figuring out who she would have been if me and the kids hadn't interrupted her destiny.

"Haven't you read any of my books?" I asked, but it was a stupid question. I always told people I wasn't the fictional characters in my novels, and now I was asking my wife to find me in those very characters. Adrianna flashed through my mind, standing by the bed, the contrast between her white panties and brown skin as she watched herself in the mirror.

I asked my wife, "Who is the man who answered the phone when I called from Alaska?"

"You probably called the wrong number."

"I don't think so. Was Mr. Matson here? It sounded like his voice."

"Carl?" she asked.

"Yes, Carl."

She appeared to search her memory. "I believe Carl came over to fix the toilet in our bedroom."

"What was wrong with the toilet?" I asked.

"The same thing that's been wrong with the toilet for two years. If you would stay busy, Aaron, maybe you wouldn't think so much about colonies in Alaska, and manifestos, and other silly things." She took the last sip of her thick magic juice and left the table.

Michelle would never go to Alaska. She would never leave our town, or the Neighborhood Wives' Club, or her middle-aged all-white tennis team. If I went to Alaska, I'd go alone.

The house became very quiet. A storm rumbled in the distance. I stood outside in the dark on the front steps staring at the Matson house. The third glass of whiskey made me feel the need to see the white airplane in the manicured green backyard. Just get a closer look. Jot down the number on the tail. Maybe peek inside.

I walked across the street in my robe and bare feet. If confronted, I'd say I was chasing off a cat that wouldn't stop meowing by the bedroom window. A big yellow cat with a baby-blue collar.

I opened the latch on the wooden gate and stepped into the backyard. I waited patiently for my eyes to adjust. For the outline of the white plane to melt back into focus.

I stared and squinted my eyes. Nothing. There was no outline of a white plane. It was gone. The yard was empty, but as I continued to stare, an object, a dark object maybe twenty feet in front of me, began to appear.

I couldn't trust my vision in the darkness. The clouds covered the moon. The light from the house next door was muted.

I tilted my head and stooped down. The blur was the approximate size of a chair, but lower to the ground. Solid. As I struggled to see the object, I heard a low guttural growl.

It was a goddamned Chow. A solid, black, barrel-chested, purple-tongued Chow in the Matsons' backyard where the white airplane was supposed to be. And before I could speak a word, the black blur rushed me, his teeth glowing like neon Halloween Dracula teeth. The crazy son of a bitch bit my knee like a ham hock. Again I found myself running wildly, slamming the wooden gate behind me, hobbling across the street to safety with the blood running down my leg, piercing hot pain shooting upward.

Inside my house I explored the damage. It wasn't as bad as it felt, barely breaking the skin, but I wrapped it up and covered the cut in white ointment to kill the dog-mouth bacteria. What kind of dog doesn't bark? What kind of domesticated animal lies in wait, seeing perfectly in the dark night, and then attacks without warning? I crawled into the small bed in the spare bedroom and finally fell asleep to the sound of raindrops on the roof. I hoped the Chow was wet and cold. He deserved it.

Sometime in the middle of the night I felt Sara crawl in bed with me. The sounds of the storm woke her, and the girl found me in the spare bedroom.

"Daddy, the lightning is loud," she whispered, folding herself into a warm spot beside me.

"You don't need to be scared. The sound you hear is thunder. It's the sound lightning makes when the air claps back together after the lightning splits open the sky. When the thunder comes, the scary part is already over."

A flash miles away lit up the room, and I counted the miles. "One, two, three, four, five, six."

The far-off thunder rumbled and rolled, Sara pushing her little face into the space under my arm. She must have roamed the house looking for me. The spare bedroom wouldn't be the first place she'd go. She probably went to the master bedroom first and chose not to crawl in bed with her mother. Chose me in a storm.

"When I was your age, I used to go to the beach sometimes with my grandfather. And sometimes we would find a sea bean."

"What's a sea bean?" Sara asked.

"It's a smooth, dark brown bean, about the size of a peanut-butter cup. They float around the ocean from places like South America and wash up on beaches far away. My grandfather believed they were wishing beans. He believed we could make a wish on the bean and it would come true."

Sara was silent, and then she said, "I wish I had one now."

"I brought one home for you," I said. "Stay here and I'll get it."

I moved through the dark house and brought the bean back to Sara. Without turning on the light, I placed it in her little hand and rubbed her fingertips on the smooth surface. She held it up and touched the bean to the soft skin of her cheek.

"It's like a stone from a river," she said.

The rain fell hard against the window, blowing sideways in the nighttime storm. We were safe and dry inside.

"Can I make a wish?" she asked.

"Yeah. You have to hold it up to your mouth and whisper the wish so no one else can hear it."

"Will it really come true?" she asked.

Sara couldn't see me smile above her.

"Maybe," I said.

When she whispered, I covered my ears so I couldn't hear the wish. A part of me wanted to know, but a bigger part of me wanted her wish to come true.

We all went to the tennis club for dinner. It was Sara's idea. She seemed to need the entire family in the same room together.

Every person who passed our table nodded or said hello to Michelle. I didn't recognize most of them. They were cute and sassy with very expensive cars and colorful visors on their clean heads. I had the distinct feeling each of them privately held the other members of the club in a higher status and lived with the subtle fear of being exposed as an imposter.

Denise stopped and said, "Michelle, where have you been, girl? We have to sign up for the doubles tournament. I can't play with Rachel again. Don't ask me to explain why, I just can't do it."

I wondered at the secret she kept, the one she was afraid of the most. The abortion in the summer before her senior year in high school. The alcoholic father. Not the romantic alcoholic in books and movies, but the disgusting alcoholic. Violent. Smelly. Dead at forty.

"We can win this year," Denise said. "Judy's out. She twisted her ankle. Oh hey, Aaron. How are you? You have the most polite children. And beautiful."

Michelle stared from across the table, her eyes begging me not to embarrass her at the club. I was a source of pride. She was the wife of a bestselling author, her identity partially determined by the worthiness of being provided for by such a man. But from Michelle's face, I could see I'd become *her* secret. The secret she was afraid would reveal itself and bring an abrupt end to her world. Maybe I was getting a little big around the middle. Spending too much time in my robe. Becoming a middle-aged angry man who should care more about next month's doubles tournament than saving the world.

"I'm fine," I said. "I'm thinking seriously about moving to Alaska. Doing my part to save the human race from extinction."

"Extinction?" Denise said. "Like the polar bears?"

"Yes, like the polar bears," I answered.

She nodded and we held eye contact a moment beyond normal.

Denise turned to point at Michelle. "You, girl—doubles, sign up tonight," and then she swished away toward the lighted green clay courts beyond the windows.

Sara said, "She smells like apricots."

"Yes, as a matter of a fact, I believe she does," I said.

"These chicken fingers are gross," Brad mumbled.

I started to argue the point, but there was no reason. I'd watched the kid eat ten thousand chicken fingers, all virtually the same, and complain about half of them. I still held hope he would eventually emerge from the instinctive fear of anything new, but in the meantime I couldn't afford to give a shit whether or not these particular chicken fingers met his criteria. My annoyance with the entire civilization was beyond safe, and the dog bite throbbed under the table.

Even after taking a moment to reason, and even after convincing myself not to confront Brad over his whining, I watched my hand reach out to Brad's plate, pick up a large untouched chicken finger, and sling it across the room like a Frisbee, bouncing off the wall beneath a painting of a sailboat caught in a storm. The chicken finger came to rest at the base of a sliding-glass door.

My family looked at me like insane men have been looked at since the beginning of time. A look of surprise, followed closely by uncertainty, and then a hint of fear. My wife didn't move a single muscle, trying her best not to draw further attention. Brad looked from me to the lonely chicken finger on the floor, and then back again several times, perhaps trying to reinforce what he'd just seen.

Sara began to laugh. Not a fake laugh like little kids sometimes do as a diversion or because they don't know what else to do, but a real laugh. Small at first. Almost indiscernible, and then quietly to herself until tears ran down her cheeks. It was funny to see a chicken finger fly across the restaurant. It was funny to watch the meat smack against the cream-colored wall, leaving a small greasy stain.

Michelle didn't find it the least bit funny. I wondered why there would be such a gulf between what a pure six-year-old thinks is hilarious and what a middle-aged woman, fully ingrained in society, finds humorous. Thirty years is a long time.

There was not a lot of talking on the way home, which was okay with me. I'd run out of things to say anyway. Every few minutes I'd hear Sara in the backseat giggle to herself, prompting Brad to whack her on the leg like she shouldn't be laughing at such a thing. Like she was an idiot for not recognizing the sure signs of family collapse.

The first thing I noticed when we pulled into the dark driveway was the open front door. It was only cracked, but the openness was out of place. It made the entire front of the house look different somehow, and I felt the adrenaline rise inside my blood. I stopped the car short of the garage.

"Did you leave the door open?" I asked.

Michelle looked. "No."

I turned my head around to the backseat. "Did either of you accidently leave the door open?"

Michelle interjected, "I remember locking it. I remember."

The inside of the car was quiet. Four sets of eyes watched the door, like maybe there was a good explanation, and if we waited long enough a well-dressed older woman would come through the door and explain. We'd all sigh with relief and then go inside where we belonged.

But no one came to the door. It just stayed cracked.

I backed down the driveway and parked the car in the street in front of the house.

"I'm gonna go inside and make sure everything's all right."

Michelle looked at me and then back to the door.

"Maybe the wind blew it open," Brad said.

"Maybe there's a tiger in there," Sara explained. "A big tiger escaped from the zoo."

"That's stupid," Brad said.

I opened the car door and started to walk across the grass to the porch. I glanced back at my wife and children watching through the windows and the Matsons' house across the street, still dark and scary.

The door was open two or three inches, but I couldn't see any pry marks or obvious signs of a problem. I pushed it open quietly and listened. The foyer seemed untouched. Maybe Brad was right. Maybe it wasn't closed all the way. A gust of wind did the trick.

I moved slowly from the foyer to the living room. It was no gust of wind. A lamp was smashed next to the couch, the cord twisted around the base, a strange oily smell.

Someone had entered our house. Drawers were pulled out and emptied. Clothes littered the bedroom floor. Sara's television had a hole busted through the screen. The mirror in our bathroom was cracked in the middle. Like someone stood and punched themselves in the reflection of their own face.

As the fear of an intruder still present in the house subsided, it was replaced in equal increments by anger. Our home was invaded. People looked through our things and picked what they wanted. They stood in my children's rooms, breaking our memories. Their eyes on our lives without permission.

It was a long walk back to the car, and an even longer wait for the police. Michelle stood in the hall and cried when she saw the broken framed pictures of the children along the bottom of the wall. It looked as though someone found pleasure in flipping each picture, one by one, and watching them crash to the floor.

The police took photographs before we could clean it away.

"Have you seen anybody suspicious around the neighborhood?" one officer asked me while we stood on the porch alone.

"No, not really," I said, half listening.

"We've had reports the last few nights about someone sneaking around this area," he said.

I couldn't seem to shake the anger. The feeling nothing would ever be the same in my house again. We could never feel safe. How could we?

"A man," the officer said, "in a robe, across the street."

"A robe?" I asked.

"Yeah," he said. "You see anybody like that?"

I looked away. "No. Maybe it wasn't a prowler. Maybe it was just somebody taking out the trash or something."

The officer glanced across the street. "I don't think so. He was seen roaming around the Matsons' backyard."

"The Matsons?" I asked.

The officer seemed to study me. "Yeah, the Matsons. Carl asked us to keep our eye on his house while they're out of town. It just seems more than coincidence. We get reports of a strange man in the neighborhood, and the next night your house is burglarized. Does anyone else have a key?"

I didn't answer his question. Mostly to myself, but loud enough for him to hear, I said, "It's a fucked-up world, wouldn't you say? When a man can take his family to dinner and come back to find his home destroyed?"

He'd seen the frustration before, maybe even felt it himself.

"Is anything missing?" he asked.

"My wife says they stole her antique silver. They also got a jar of quarters and dimes I kept in the closet."

"Probably kids," he said. Like it made everything better, knowing the people who trashed my house and stole our security were juveniles. Somebody's children. Children who thought it was acceptable to go through a house and knock family pictures to the floor, leaving shattered glass under our feet.

Long after the police left and we cleaned up the best we could, I sat out on the front porch alone. After almost an hour, Sara came outside in her pajamas carrying a little blanket and sat down next to me on the wooden bench. She rested her head against my arm.

"Are you okay?" I asked.

"It would've been better if it was a tiger," she said.

I thought about it. "Why?" I asked.

"Because a tiger doesn't know better."

She was right. I hadn't thought about it that way. The horrible feeling inside us caused by the invasion of our home, our place of safety, was rooted deep in the knowledge that humans had done it to us, against the natural law not to destroy for the sake of destruction, not to hurt for pleasure. If it had been animals, we could have cleaned up and forgotten. But people broke through our doors, dirtied our sanctity on purpose for a jar of grimy coins. And maybe they'd come back. Maybe the door would be open every time we came home.

"They stole my wishing bean," Sara said in a whisper.

I looked out across the yard. It needed cutting.

"Maybe it's just lost."

"No, I put it in the jewelry box. The robbers took the whole box with the bean inside."

I could feel her sadness pressing against my body, literally feel it melt into me. A child's sadness. Soft and unsure. Not complicated by reasons or motives.

"Well," I said, "it's a good thing you already made your wish. A bean only has one good wish in it for each person. After that, it's not good for much."

She was quiet for a time.

"But my wish didn't come true, Daddy."

I reached my hand around and touched her face.

"What did you wish for?"

"I wished George would like me."

"George?"

"Yes."

"Isn't he the stupid kid in your class you wanted to move away?"

"That was a long time ago," she said. "He's not stupid anymore."

"Oh."

After a while I thought Sara had fallen asleep against me. The moon was bright above, and I looked for movement in the Matsons' dark windows.

Sara asked, "How come lightning makes such a terrible loud noise, but when a giant star burns out and disappears forever, somebody's sun, we can't hear anything at all? It just goes away quiet."

I must have taken too long to answer, because when I finally thought of something to say, Sara was asleep, her breathing steady and heavy, and I didn't get a chance to tell her about the death of a distant star.

The invasion of our home and the reminder of life's insecurity created a new dynamic within my family. After Sara fell asleep with me on the porch, I carried her gently to her bedroom, but something wouldn't allow me to leave the child alone. I checked and rechecked the doors, knowing full well our intruder might have a key to every lock protecting my children from the evil outside.

Eventually, I placed Sara in the master bed between me and Michelle. I couldn't fall asleep, analyzing every noise, listening for the sound of a key in a lock, door hinges, a tiger on the threshold.

Michelle reached over our daughter in the darkness and touched my shoulder. It was the first time we'd physically touched since I'd been home from Alaska, if you don't count the wooden kiss in the kitchen upon my arrival.

Her hand didn't stay on my shoulder long, maybe five seconds, but it meant a great deal. In just the few short hours since I'd hurled a chicken finger across the country club, things had changed. We were given the insight of a shaken foundation. The opportunity to acknowledge our taking for granted. Before the night was over, all four of us were in the same bed, snoring and kicking each other in fits of wakeful dreams.

I was running out of days before I had to make up my mind and travel back to Alaska for an appearance before the Committee. I was a bit surprised not to have heard yet from Bryan, or Adrianna, or even the mysterious man on the porch at the mountain cabin. The silence could mean anything, or nothing at all.

The next morning I was informed by Michelle that the Neighborhood Wives' Club would be meeting at our home for dinner. In my absence, Michelle had been elected to a position called financial trustee.

"Is that the same as treasurer?" I asked.

"No, it's not," she answered.

"Well, what do you do?" I asked.

"I keep up with the Club finances, make sure we stay under budget, write checks sometimes."

I couldn't resist. "Like a treasurer," I said.

"No," she answered again. "Like a financial trustee."

I couldn't help but revisit my dream with Rita Blanchard and the doctor's wife, Cindy Sheerer, loading Civil War muskets and taking shots at each other from their pretty green lawns. The rough metal ball would explode into bone and blood, ripping the woman's chest-flesh into brutal shards of skin and meat. The matter would be settled Neighborhood Wives' style, refined and absolute, in a Civil War kind of way.

The kids were smart enough to find friends' houses to spend the night out. I planned to sit on the front porch with a small cooler to mix icy cocktails and let my imagination spin with the idea of Jamestown, Alaska. Find out where my notes and outline would go. Maybe the story could be written from the inside out, through the eyes of someone like the Mongolian. Outside of the Committee, but a member of the colony. For all I knew, maybe the Mongolian was the king of the whole place, the head of the snake, the brains behind the decolonization of a dying world.

I took my spot on the front porch as the women began to arrive one by one. Some chatty and comfortable, others dressed for battle with ridiculous self-indulgent outfits.

I am not sure exactly why—there was no certain conversation or glance—but I began to feel each of these women possessed a certain nibblet of information they deemed important about me, or my life, or maybe the world in general. Information they believed I would desperately want to know, and so our conversations were stilted and odd, even odder than usual.

Rita Blanchard showed no ill effects from the information she possessed.

"Well, hello, Aaron Jennings. I thought you were dead."

"No, not dead. Just out of town."

She lingered by the front door, watching me. She was different than the other wispy-thin, fair-skinned women. Rita Blanchard must have had a little gypsy blood. Her hair was black and her hips formidable. There was something behind the smile.

"You know, Aaron, a woman comes alive with good music and comfortable shoes," she said for no apparent reason, and then waited for an answer.

"I'll remember that, Rita," I said. "And by the way, stay away from muskets."

She smiled like she was familiar with my dream, which she couldn't possibly have been, so I smiled back like an idiot, and she went away, finally leaving me alone. All of the members of the Club were safely inside the clubhouse, sipping white wine and making big decisions.

It all made me miss Adrianna. Alive and wild. The opposite of the women inside the house behind my back. Except maybe Rita Blanchard. I could imagine her alive and wild once, maybe still.

There was no way for me to call Adrianna. There was no way to hear her voice before I'd go back to Alaska. Maybe it was better. A cleaner decision, uncomplicated by animal desires. I could weigh lofty ideals and family obligations as purely as such things can be weighed without obsessing over whether particular angles might include being naked with particular women.

The level of noise inside the house would rise and fall like spectators at a golf match, a loud roar followed by complete silence. As the evening became night, I fixed another drink and began to ponder the mystery of my key.

It didn't fit the front door or the back door of my house. Why not? I'd never had trouble with it before. And then, a few days after arriving home, someone enters my house apparently using a key, no forced entry.

Without making too much noise, I tried my key once again in the lock of my front door and once again it failed to work. The locks didn't appear new. They were the same old locks we always had, and the key looked the same, maybe worn down a bit, but certainly it wouldn't stop working in both locks at the same time.

I sat back down and touched my lips to the rim of the cool glass, fixing my eyes on the house across the street. The house of Carl Matson. The officer said they were out of town. Nobody was home. What if, for some strange reason, the key on my keychain opened the front door of the Matsons' house instead of mine? What would that mean? Why would I even think about such a possibility? But the very fact the idea crossed my mind at all made it somehow realistic. Maybe not so crazy. Not any crazier than spy drones, black Chows, one-legged birds, or stolen wishing beans.

The neighborhood was quiet and empty. Most of the husbands were taking advantage of the opportunity, playing poker elsewhere, watching a game at the sports bar. The Matson house was dark again, and I knew I was one drink away from sticking my key in their lock and praying it wouldn't turn. And as I predicted, one drink later I was sneaking around the neighborhood like a goofy kid until I found myself at the front door of Mr. and Mrs. Carl Matson's lovely ranch-style home.

There was darkness inside. As before, the only light came from the muted green numbers of the digital clock on the stove. I heard a roar of laughter rise from my house and then subside. I pulled the keychain from my pocket and held it up between my eyes and the streetlight to pick the correct key.

I looked left and then right, probably much like the prowler the night before looked left and right as he entered my door and took from us far more than a few coins and trinkets. But this was different. I imagined myself on a mission.

The key slid gently into the lock. I started to turn slowly, hoping it would catch. Hoping it would stop vertical. The wrong key in the wrong lock. But it didn't stop. The key turned easily, and I heard the bolt slide.

My key, the key on my key ring, fit the Matsons' front door. And somewhere, someone else had my key.

I turned my back to the door and scanned the neighborhood. The Wives' meeting was in full swing. I could see women through the open kitchen window moving briskly, wine glasses in hand, big joyful smiles.

If the Matsons were out of town, surely the alarm would be set. If I opened the door it would activate and I'd have thirty seconds before everyone in the neighborhood heard the screeching noise and the police descended on me like a caged rat.

I devised a plan. A good one, I believed. I would open the door a few inches, run back across the street to my cocktail, wait two or three minutes, and if the alarm didn't sound and no police flew into the neighborhood, I'd come back to the door in the darkness.

And there I sat, sipping a watered-down drink and acting as casual as any man sitting on his porch in the evening and listening to the cackles of intoxicated white women a wall away.

Nobody came. The night was quiet other than the tinkling of ice in my upturned glass and the murmurs of women's voices. I circled down the block and came back to the Matsons' front door. Still open just a crack, as I'd left it.

Now I faced the question of what to do. Lock the door tight and walk away, go home and think about things? Or go inside, look around, put to rest the mystery of Carl Matson once and for all.

I pushed the door. It swung slowly open a few feet. The light from the street glowed through the front windows. I peeked into the dining room and squinted my eyes to adjust to the change. I was halfway in and halfway out, no place to be, and stepped inside finally, closing the door gently behind me.

I felt the rush of a burglar. There I stood in another family's house, looking for God knew what, but pulled along by curiosity, maybe even paranoia and delusion infused with a touch of whiskey. It didn't matter now. I was where I was.

I left the dining room and entered a neat kitchen. There was nothing to suggest anyone was home. The green digital clock showed 9:21. Maybe I should check the garage to see if the white plane was hidden inside. I moved through the kitchen into the darker living room, separated from the glow of the streetlights. There was a sliding-glass door facing the backyard, and I stood there trying to detect the slightest movement outside, the shadowy pacing of a Chow in the grass. My back was to the living room, and in the absolute silence I heard the smallest of sounds behind me.

It came from the aqua-green couch I'd seen before, next to the table with the lamp. Such a small sound. Imperceptible in a regular moment. But this was no regular moment. I was in the midst of a felony, standing in another man's home, violating his life the way I'd been violated the night before. I didn't turn around, just waited. Waited either for another sound or a viable explanation for the first sound.

Seconds passed. I could feel my body inhale and then exhale, my chest expanding with each breath. The voice behind me said, "The dog is gone."

I whirled around to face the couch as the lamp suddenly illuminated the room. Bryan's hand lowered from inside the shade, and he sat with a wry smile in one of his trademark sweaters, charcoal grey.

"You scared the shit outta me," I said.

I moved away from the glass door. I was angry, too angry to deal yet with the complexity of the situation.

"What are you doing here?" I asked, as if it was my house he'd entered again without permission. As if it was my couch he occupied in the dark.

"I guess I could ask you the same question."

"Jesus," I said. "You could've given me a heart attack. I knew Matson was mixed up in all this. I knew it."

Bryan kept the same smile. "Aaron, you don't know what you know yet."

My anger began to dissipate, and the strangeness of the circumstances filled the room like smoke.

"Aaron, there's only one real question. Have you decided what you want to do?"

I blurted out, "Why do you want me so bad? There's a million writers out there, why me?"

Bryan's face settled into a more serious expression.

"That's a valid question, I suppose, but I'm not prepared to give you the answer. It doesn't matter. You have the opportunity of a lifetime, Aaron. Whether we succeed or fail, you, and you alone, will choose the words that will define history.

"Think about it—and I know you already have. Think about that power. Words are power. The way you choose to describe our movement will persuade or dissuade people around the world.

"It's a big deal, and you're the best person for the job. The right person, with the right talent, at the exact right point in the history of human civilization."

I looked at him sitting on the couch. How long had he been there? How did he know I would come? Hell, I didn't even know I'd come until just minutes before I decided.

"How did you get in here?" I asked. "I was across the street on my porch watching since before it was dark."

Bryan smiled again. "You're not focusing on the big picture, Aaron. What difference does it make how I got in here?

"Listen—this world is divided into givers and takers. Most of us fall somewhere in the middle, just a little over the line one way or the other. But some people, like that woman parked in the handicapped spot, or the two guys who broke into your house. They're takers. Defined by their taking. From me, you, the government, their parents, bosses, landlords, their own children. Doesn't matter. They don't understand self-sufficiency, independence, the beauty of hard work and the satisfaction of its rewards. They never will. Instead, they'll take, and take, and take, and take, until they've taken your last breath, our last breath, every ounce of goodness from this world.

"People used to be afraid mankind would kill itself with big bombs or a laboratory virus. It's much less sensational. Misplaced intentions will do the job from the inside out.

"We've rotted, Aaron, morally to the core. This may be our last opportunity to save what's left before the takers take it all."

His words were unnaturally convincing, as they'd always been. I felt almost like God Himself was calling me to battle.

Before I could speak, there was the faint sound of a siren in the distance. I listened, again feeling the air enter and leave my chest, and stared at Bryan, waiting for any reaction.

The sound of the siren got closer and closer, until I knew it was only a few blocks from turning into my subdivision. Had somebody called the police? Did the light in the living room alert an elderly neighbor? Was there a silent alarm?

The siren turned the corner, but Bryan held his position. They were close. I could see the reflection of blue lights through the kitchen window. There was no time to wait. No place to be caught. So I turned, unlocked the sliding-glass door, and ran through the backyard, turning around just before I jumped the fence to see Bryan still sitting on the aqua couch next to the lamp, his expression the same as it had been when I left the room.

I climbed the fence, circling through the Thompsons' backyard, down to the edge of the woods. The sirens seemed to come from all directions, lights reflecting throughout the neighborhood.

I felt like a fugitive, breathing hard, my senses heightened, completely sober. As I emerged onto the road, the sirens began to fade away. The spinning lights off in pursuit of another.

I made my way back to the spot on my front porch and sat down. The Matsons' house was dark again. Our front door opened, and Rita Blanchard appeared on the porch, closing the door behind her. She was looser than before, the wine changing the shape of her face.

"Okay, Mr. Jennings, you'll have your house back in a few minutes. The party's almost over."

I could feel the sweat on my forehead and under my arms. Rita Blanchard noticed. "You look a little nervous, Aaron."

I chose not to say anything, but instead began preparing myself another drink from the cooler. Like I was too busy to engage in conversation.

She said, with a certain degree of smugness, "Well, if I was you, I'd be nervous, too."

Holding a handful of ice cubes, I looked up at her. What exactly did she mean? What did all of them know?

"My husband's leaving for Peru on business," she said. "If you get a chance, stop by tomorrow night for a drink. I need to ask you something."

With the ice melting in my hand, I watched Rita Blanchard walk slowly home past the Matsons' house, her body swaying to the music in her head, her shoes probably extremely comfortable. I hadn't the slightest idea what to do.

I walked around in the dilemma of indecision from day to day. I would reach the point where my mind was made up, and then a few minutes later doubt would creep like a sloth from the shadows of my cranium. Go to Alaska, or stay at home?

But it wasn't black and white. I could come back any time I wanted, right? My family could move to Alaska any time they decided. A lot would depend on the success or failure of the experiment, the movement, whatever the hell it was.

I would miss my routine. I would miss Sara and Brad, and probably even Michelle. But if I turned down this job (I had begun to see it as a job offer), would I forever wish I hadn't? Would I wish at least I'd taken a few months to watch it all unfold? And what about Adrianna, and my publisher's deadline, and getting four out of seven Committee votes?

If I decided not to accept the position, it only seemed right for me to fly back to Alaska anyway and tell the Committee in person. Give them an explanation. After all, I'd been chosen from a world of writers. And if I decided to accept the position, maybe I could call it temporary. Tell everyone at home I was going into seclusion to finish a novel I couldn't finish at the house. Lay around naked with Adrianna for a few months drinking wine like Bacchus.

The phone rang. It was my editor, Susan. She liked to call on Sundays.

"Tell me you've got two hundred fifty pages," she said immediately.

So I said, "I've got two hundred fifty pages."

"Really?"

"No, not really."

As always, her voice kind of drifted like she was looking around her desk for something important.

"How many do you have?" she asked.

"Susan, I'm thinkin' about taking some time off. A sabbatical. Go up to Alaska. Maybe find a remote cabin. Write a different book."

There was a pause, long and hard.

"That's not a good idea, Aaron."

"Why not?"

"Different books don't sell. We've had this conversation before. Your fans know what they love, and they know what to expect when they buy an Aaron Jennings novel."

Her voice became direct and purposeful.

"Aaron, we've got a deadline. The monkeys are hungry. I need to see what you've written so far."

"It's a mess. I need a few days to put it together."

She seemed to smell my lie. The woman had been an editor for twenty-five years. She'd been lied to before.

"Give me a hint," she said. "What's it about?"

From where I stood in the kitchen wearing my favorite white robe, I could see the Matsons' house across the street. I could see the door I'd snuck through the night before.

I said, "It's about a man who lives in a nice, suburban neighborhood with his wife and children. He starts to notice strange things happening in the house across the street, a house he believed was occupied by a retired couple who mostly cared about keeping their yard pretty.

"Anyway, eventually the man's imagination, paranoia, mixed with real events, leads him to break into the neighbors' house while they're out of town."

"Yeah?" she said, breathing into the receiver.

"He finds something bad in the closet," I said.

"What's he find the closet?" she asked.

"I don't know yet, Susan. Something bad."

"Maybe a body," she offered. "Or his chopped-up wife? What about a deformed child? A grown, deformed child, kept in the closet, who sneaks out and mutilates people, or cattle, or something like that."

I was tired of the conversation. "How 'bout he finds a book in the closet?" I said. "A little red book. *The Survival Manifesto*. The seed that changed the world."

There was another pause.

"I don't understand," she said.

"Neither do I, Susan. I just know I don't feel like writing the same damn story again and again, whether I stay here and sip coffee or go to Alaska. I just can't do it right now."

She'd talked writers off the ledge before. There was no panic in her voice. I pictured Susan, shaking her head from side to side mocking me to the colleague across her desk as they shared a knowing smile. The smile of the intelligentsia.

"Are we having a little midlife crisis?" she asked.

Across the street, through the kitchen widow, I watched Rita Blanchard approach the Matsons' front door, insert a key, and disappear inside. I stepped closer to the window and maneuvered my head to see through the cracks in the blinds.

"Probably so," I said. "I love your idea about the deformed son in the closet. I'll use it," and I hung up.

My eyes stayed glued to the Matsons' house while the phone rang and rang. After a few minutes, Rita exited, locked the door behind her, and headed down the sidewalk.

The phone stopped ringing and started again. I picked it up.

"My midlife crisis is over," I said.

Another female voice, not Susan's, said, "That's an interesting way to answer the phone."

"Adrianna?"

"Aaron?" she said, and giggled.

Her voice was so soft and delightful. The effect on my body was instantaneous, like a drug, sunshine, a gentle breeze. I don't remember even worrying about the fact she'd called me at home.

"Why didn't you come see me before I left?" I asked.

"It was too risky. We weren't supposed to bother you while you were making your decision. Are you coming back?" she said.

"I'm supposed to go before the Committee for a vote," I said, stepping around the issue of whether or not I'd reached a final decision. "Do you think I've got the votes?"

"A lot's happened since you left. Bryan says the swing vote is Lei. We've talked to her. Everybody wants something."

"What does Lei want?" I asked.

There was a sound in the background.

"I have to go," Adrianna whispered. "I can't wait till you get here. Stacey will pick you up tomorrow at 9 a.m."

The phone went dead.

How did Bryan know about the lady parking in the handicapped spot? How did he know it was two men who broke into my house? Maybe there was no Mr. Matson. Maybe the house was used to watch me for the months or even years leading up to the day Bryan appeared on the back porch with his proposal.

I tried to remember when the Matsons moved in. At least two years. How was Rita Blanchard involved? What did Adrianna do for Lei's vote?

Sara sat down beside me on the back porch on a nice afternoon. She fit perfectly in the space between my body and the arm of the wicker chair.

"Can I ask you a question?" she began.

"You can ask me anything in the world, and I'll try to give you an answer."

"I watched a science show on TV. They said the sun is gonna burn out in five billion years. Can we live here without the sun?"

"Well, no. But five billion years is a long time," I said.

I could tell the wheels were turning in her little mind.

She said, "Do you think people will be smart enough in five billion years to build a new sun?"

It was a very good question. I didn't know the answer.

"I hope so, Sara," I said.

We were quiet for a time. "Me, too," she said softly to herself. "I hope so, too."

I wasn't sure what to do about the Rita Blanchard invitation, but after watching her enter the Matsons' house, I knew I had to go.

Just after dark, I told Michelle I was taking a walk around the block. I looked a bit silly in the mirror with the shorts and tennis shoes, my body slowly morphing into the body of a middle-aged man who doesn't earn a living with his hands. I needed a haircut. The remnants of the Chow bite were still visible on my knee.

I kept a keen eye out for cars and other walkers. Rita Blanchard's house was pitch black. There wasn't a light inside or out. I walked past her driveway casually two or three hundred yards before turning around.

Standing at the Blanchards' front door, I could smell incense. A sweet patchouli aroma, heavy and nauseating. I knocked softly.

It remained dark inside, but I could hear noises in the house. The door opened quickly and Rita stood before me.

"What are you doing here?" she said.

Her manner was brusque. She was in the middle of something, her hair strangely

lopsided. The best I could tell, she was wearing a large dress that looked remarkably like a Mexican blanket, with bright colors and fringe.

I stuttered, "You…you asked me to stop by…for a drink. You said you had something to tell me."

There was a noise behind Rita. Someone else was in the house. We looked at each other for a peculiar period of time.

Rita said, "Things aren't always as they seem, Aaron."

That was it. We both just continued to stare at each other three feet apart, me in my shorts and old-man body, Rita wearing a colorful Mexican blanket.

"That's it?" I said. "That's what you wanted to tell me? 'Things aren't always the way they seem'?"

Without any expression whatsoever on her face, she closed the door and left me standing by myself.

I couldn't seem to walk away.

"No shit," I said to nobody. "Things aren't always the way they seem. That's good to know. Maybe you could have said, 'Things are never the way they seem.' That would've been more accurate. Maybe even worth walking down the block to hear."

Still standing at the door, still talking to no one, I repeated, "Things aren't always the way they seem. Is your husband really in Peru? Are you and Bryan rolling around the kitchen floor naked, surrounded by patchouli? Five billion years can't come soon enough."

The house was quiet when I arrived home. Michelle was sitting in the bed reading a magazine.

"How was your walk?" she asked.

"Weird," I answered. "Everything's weird. The world is weird. Don't you think?"

Michelle said, "I think the world is pretty neutral. It's the people in it who are weird."

I thought about that as I changed shirts.

"You're probably right. By the way, I've gotta fly back to Alaska tomorrow for book stuff again."

"How long will you be there?" she asked.

"I'm not sure. I'll call and let you know."

I crawled into bed and lay still with my back toward my wife. My eyes were open. Every minute or so she'd flip a page of the magazine.

The lamp finally turned off, and I felt Michelle scoot in my direction and position herself against me. It felt like I remembered before, and I could smell her, feel her breasts pressed against my back.

Why, I thought. *Why now? What switch inside her woman brain made her crawl across the bed for the first time in so many months to touch me? What instinct told her?*

Michelle's hand rested on my hip, and then found its way slowly down to the elastic top of my underwear and beyond. Strangely, my guilt over Adrianna had no effect whatsoever on the erection that rose and fell under my wife's hand.

THE COMMITMENT

On Monday morning, two hours before my scheduled departure, I sat with Sara at the kitchen table for our regular pre-school routine. She crunched her unnaturally crunchy cereal and I sipped my coffee between turning the pages of the newspaper.

"Guess what?" she said.

"What?"

"George likes me. The wishin' bean worked. One day he didn't like me, and the next day he did. Just like that."

She snapped her fingers, something I'm sure she learned from one of those hypnotic TV shows on the kids' channel. Sara smiled. I had a flash of my girl all grown up, diluted by the world.

"And this is the guy you told me was stupid?" I asked.

She took a huge spoonful of cereal. "That was a long time ago, Dad."

"This is the guy you told me couldn't help being stupid, because that's just the way God made him, and now, you've got one wish, guaranteed to come true, anything in the universe, and you wish for the stupid guy to like you."

"And it worked. And next week, if I have another wishin' bean, I might use it to wish for somethin' else. Maybe world peace, or a cure for cancer, or ice cream."

She still had the fresh mind of a six-year-old, but it was decomposing quickly. Three more years, maybe four, and she'd be sure I was an idiot.

"Don't you think some of those things are more important than others?" I asked.

She looked up from the cereal, blue eyes bright, ponytail hanging down in the back. "No," she said. "They're all the same."

In a flash we said goodbye, and the children were out the door to school. I was left with the article on page four.

> Anne Marie Crockett, age 36, was charged Thursday with the murder of her two-year-old son, Andrew, after the child's decomposing body was found in the woman's bed.
>
> The child apparently refused to say "Amen" after the Sunday dinner prayer and was denied food and water as punishment until he eventually died of dehydration. The mother, a member of a small church known as the Communal Society of God's Children, told authorities she believed the Devil had entered her son's mouth and wouldn't allow him to speak the word "Amen." Starvation was the only means to drive out the beast and save Andrew.
>
> After the boy's death he was placed on the mother's bed while members of the church gathered around to pray for his resurrection. Instead of rising from the dead, the boy's body began to decompose until the police received an anonymous call from a concerned church member who was afraid the prayers were not effective.
>
> Crockett is being held without bond in jail and has thus far refused to consult with attorneys appointed by the court. She has requested the child's burial be delayed to allow additional time for her son to come back to life and the murder charges to be dismissed.

On the same page, a few inches below, my eye caught the headline BIGFOOT BODY A HOAX. Two men in Oregon claimed to have found a dead Bigfoot body on a riverbank deep in the Oregon forest. The beast had apparently simply died of natural causes while sipping cool, fresh rainwater, perhaps the victim of high cholesterol or a bad heart.

The body turned out to be nothing but a stuffed gorilla suit encased in ice. When asked why he would perpetrate such a hoax, Ed Weber (age forty-nine) said, "We wanted to find a Bigfoot body so bad, I think we convinced ourselves we had. It's just a matter of time."

Yes, Ed, it's just a matter of time. Everything's just a matter of time.

Later in the morning, I stood looking out the front window, impatiently waiting for Stacey to arrive and drive me to the airport. Michelle had come home after dropping the kids at school, and she was dressed in a spunky little tennis outfit. She stood next to me, and we looked out the window together as Stacey's car rolled to a stop in front of the house.

"Call me when you get there," she said.

We watched the effeminate man exit the car and saunter in our direction.

"I love you," Michelle said softly, and I believed her. It wasn't dramatic. Just a husband and wife saying goodbye for a few days, but I felt the effect of her words despite myself. A warmth.

We like to believe we're self-contained, able to provide ourselves all we need, but it isn't true. At least not for any length of time. We're weak and needy animals. Michelle's words made me feel a familiar old reassurance, sometimes lost in the daily push and pull of marriage and kids, debts and dialogue.

We hugged, and I opened the door as Stacey's fist was cocked to knock.

"Good morning, Mr. Jennings," he said, spry and excited, a caricature of himself. "Good morning, Mrs. Jennings."

As we drove away, I watched Michelle standing alone on the porch, and I waved. She waved back.

Immediately, Stacey began to babble.

"Back to Alaska, huh?"

He was wearing fingernail polish. A shiny peach shade.

"You know, I've never been there, to the new city, I mean. I pick up people and drop 'em off all over the place, but I've never been. They say it's beautiful." Before I could answer, Stacey said, "Sometimes I wonder if it really exists. I mean, what if it's like a movie set and all the people are just actors?"

I turned to look at him as he spoke.

"If you went up to touch most of the buildings, they're just 3-D paintings or digital images. It's all a big show."

Stacey stopped talking. "Why would they do that?" I asked.

"Why?" he repeated. "To trick people out of money. Sell 'em this big, grand idea of a new world order. A safe place for our children. God's plan. How much would people pay for such a thing?"

"I haven't paid a penny," I said.

"No, you haven't," he said and smiled.

"Is that funny?" I asked.

"Oh, no," he answered. "Do you know how many famous people I've driven to airports in the past five years? Businessmen, politicians, movie stars, writers?"

He stopped talking again.

"What exactly are you saying?" I asked.

The man looked at me for the first time, and we held eye contact for a few beats.

He shrugged his shoulders. "Nothing, just thinkin'—that's all."

Remarkably, we didn't speak again the entire ride to the small airport. I kept going to Jamestown in my mind. The buildings, the people.

Larry was standing outside the plane when I arrived. He wasn't as tall as I remembered, maybe because the chef's hat was nowhere to be seen.

Larry took my bag from Stacey. "This is an awfully light bag, Aaron. Is it a clue to your decision?"

"Where's your hat?" I asked.

"I don't wear it anymore. It isn't necessary now. If you plan to turn down the job, you don't need to fly all the way to Alaska to tell us. I'll pass the news along."

I told him the truth. "I haven't made up my mind, Larry."

Larry looked at Stacey, and Stacey retreated dutifully. I entered the empty plane and took the same seat against the window

No sooner had I gotten situated when another person arrived. It was the man from before, the crying man, and he sat in his familiar chair across the aisle in front of me. We nodded acknowledgments before his old, short body disappeared into the seat.

He was quiet as the plane taxied down the runway and Larry steered us into the great blue sky. I listened carefully for any crying, but the little man was silent.

At what seemed to be the right moment, I said, "Thanks for the wishin' bean."

After a pause, from the other side of the chair the man's voice said, "You're welcome. Did it work?"

"Well, actually it did. I wished the plane wouldn't crash in the bad storm, and then we landed safely. My little girl wished a stupid kid named George would like her, and he does."

The voice said, "The plane wasn't going to crash anyway, and the stupid boy doesn't really like your daughter."

I moved my head slightly to try to see a piece of the man's face, but the angle wouldn't allow it. I gave up and thought about what he said.

"How do you know?"

The voice answered, "What difference does it make how I know? You wasted your wishes. You should return the bean to me."

I actually stood from my chair and caught a glimpse of the top of his small head.

"It was stolen," I said.

The man didn't respond. I slowly sat back down. He seemed angry I couldn't produce his special bean. I waited at least five minutes before I finally said, "The last time we flew together, why were you crying?"

The voice said, "I was crying because I knew you'd waste your wishes and lose the bean. It's the cost of knowing the future, Mr. Jennings. I wouldn't wish it on the Devil himself.

"Now, if you'll excuse me, I'm going to sleep. Please don't disturb me."

I was left alone with my thoughts. If the little man knew the future, maybe he could tell me what my decision would ultimately be. I wasn't the type of person who waited until the last minute to make up my mind on something so important, but I couldn't seem to lock it down one way or the other. I kept thinking of something Bryan once said: "We're trapped by the things we love." But if we really love those things, they shouldn't be traps at all.

What did I love more? Could I have all of it at the same time? There are so many unimportant things complicating our lives, clouding the day, disguising themselves as something worthy.

My bowels began to move. Without checking the time I knew it was 11:00 a.m. The remainder of the flight was uneventful as the little man kept the future to himself.

I was greeted by the stoic Mongolian and Bryan standing beside a limousine. Bryan's face looked tired, washed out, and his trademark sweater, pale on this occasion, seemed to reflect the mood.

"Welcome home," he said to me, but before I could respond, Larry interjected, "He hasn't made up his mind."

"I see you've met Dr. Lambert," Bryan said, gesturing in the direction of the small man who'd been my companion on the flight.

"Not really," I answered.

As the Mongolian packed away our suitcases, Bryan explained, "Dr. Lambert is the head of our scientific division. He'll be hitching a ride with us to the lab."

Myself, Larry, Bryan, and Dr. Lambert climbed aboard the limousine driven by the Mongolian, who deftly avoided eye contact with me. Bryan turned his head and put something in his mouth, washing it down with a swig of bottled water. There was a messy silence, so I started a conversation.

"What goes on in the scientific division?" I asked no particular person.

Bryan answered, "Right now, the good doctor is making great strides in the field of shock treatments to cure our unfortunate brothers and sisters."

"Shock treatments? Isn't that a bit archaic?" I asked.

Dr. Lambert refused to join the conversation. He stared out the window and held a small black purse tightly in his lap.

Bryan said, "It's a little more advanced than the old-fashioned, metal-helmet shock treatments. We're looking at ways to permanently alter behavior." Bryan looked over at the side of Dr. Lambert's expressionless face. "Tell Mr. Jennings a little about your progress, Doctor."

Dr. Lambert seemed lost in his own thoughts, but the sound of his name brought him back to us. After a moment he said, "An event occurred three years ago in Australia. Quite extraordinary, actually. At the time it didn't seem like much. Three men—vagabonds, lifetime criminals, drug addicts, one a severe alcoholic—were caught in a violent rainstorm. They huddled together under a small rock overhang, riding out the storm.

"The men were struck by lightning. Not just any lightning. In layman's terms, a super-charged, horizontal bolt of lightning. A direct hit traveling sideways five feet above the ground."

Dr. Lambert told the story like he'd told it a thousand times before but still couldn't hide his enthusiasm.

"They didn't die," he said. "In fact, something phenomenal took place. The men, all three of them, showed immediate and seemingly permanent behavioral changes. They got jobs, paid their bills, refrained from immoral or criminal activity, and became sickened by the idea of drugs or alcohol. Friends and family said they were unrecognizable.

"At first, it was written off as a psychological phenomenon, just a reaction to a near-death experience, but with extensive studies we found it was something more, much more."

Dr. Lambert paused. I was intrigued. "What?" I asked.

"The lightning actually altered their DNA. For lack of a better way to explain it, strands of DNA were melted and then regenerated, growing back together, creating completely new people. People who didn't exist before that bolt of lightning shot across the ground and struck those men."

Dr. Lambert concluded, "The transformation has been permanent in all three subjects. We've been trying to duplicate the process, so far with limited success, but it's certainly worth the effort."

Larry made a sound. It was difficult to decipher, but it was most probably the sound of disapproval.

Bryan said, "Imagine if we could turn lifelong criminals, child molesters, into hardworking human beings. Imagine zapping lazy people off the couch, fat people away from the refrigerator, or drunks out of the mindset of getting behind the wheel. It's like magic."

If Dr. Lambert could see the future, then he already knew the results of his experiment. He already knew the fate of Jamestown, and his own fate, and the fate of everything hidden in the little purse clutched in his tiny lap. I imagined it full of wishing beans.

The Mongolian stopped in front of a large building with the word SCIENCE inscribed above the doors. I moved my head from side to side in an effort to make sure it wasn't just a digital image or a 3-D prop. It looked real.

Dr. Lambert and Larry exited the limousine. Through the open window, Bryan said, "We'll see you at dinner, Doctor."

As we drove to the Committee Chamber, I waited for the conversation I knew would come.

Bryan said, "Tomorrow is the big day. Your appearance before the Committee is set for ten in the morning. I still feel good about Lei's vote. Did you talk to any of the Committee members besides me while you were home?"

"No," I said, and as usual immediately regretted my lie.

"Is it true what Larry said? You haven't made up your mind yet?"

I saw the Mongolian glance at me in the rearview mirror. I didn't answer Bryan's question.

He said, "Let's have dinner. Me, you, Lambert, maybe Lei could join us."

After we arrived at our destination, the Mongolian silently led me to my old room. The halls were empty and the stout man appeared to stomp a bit harder than usual. He unlocked the door, handed me the key, and walked away without a word.

There were only four chairs at the round dinner table. When I arrived Dr. Lambert and Bryan were already enjoying glasses of dark red wine. I assumed the fourth chair was for Lei, the Asian, lesbian, genius, female swing vote. She was nowhere to be seen.

For the first time I was able to study Dr. Lambert. He was a strange looking man. Dwarflike, but in proportion. His eyes darted around the room, occasionally coming to rest on something, and he would lose himself in thought.

I said jokingly as I sat down, "Well, Dr. Lambert, did you shock a few vagabonds before dinner?" Nobody laughed, so I continued, "I've been thinking about what you said. How do you know the shock treatment with the super-charged lightning will always make people better? Maybe it was just a coincidence all three of the Australian guys were transformed into better people. Depending on what strand of DNA is melted, and how it grows back, maybe it could turn an honest man into a cold-blooded killer."

Bryan answered, "We don't shock honest men, we only shock the hopeless bastards who've proven over and over that they won't make the right decisions. They'll choose the needle over their babies, watching pornography over taking out the trash, stealing over working, lying over telling the truth. What do we have to lose? They're miserable anyway. Ask one. How could they possibly be happy?"

Dr Lambert said, "We only take volunteers."

I said, "And at the end, when their brains are mush, I imagine they don't complain much."

A handsome waiter filled our glasses. Lei's chair remained empty.

Bryan said, "What do you want me to say, Aaron? Would you like me to throw my hands in the air and announce the entire mankind experiment was a complete failure? A noisy, nasty-smelling failure? The world will be a far better place when we're gone? Extinct? Just plants and rodents left to ponder the wonder of God, and the universe, love, poetry?

"Is that what you want me to do, because I won't do it. If we don't fight, me and you, for the human race, who will, Aaron? Who's up to the task?"

The meal was excellent, the service efficient and friendly. Lei's chair stayed empty. No one mentioned the absence, but at least twice I noticed Bryan glance in the direction of the chair. Dwarflike thoughts.

After coffee, Dr. Lambert excused himself. In the quiet of the large room, Bryan leaned back in his chair, his left hand resting on the base of his wine glass, turning it slowly. I waited for him to speak.

"I know it's a difficult decision. I had to make it once myself. All of us have. The fact that it was the right thing to do didn't make it any less difficult. In some ways it made it harder. Acknowledging, truly acknowledging the sickened state of this world, the need for such desperate action, the utter darkness only a few generations away."

I listened to the words. Lei's empty chair sat like another person in the room. Bryan lifted the wine glass to his lips and took a sip. His eyelids fought the pull of gravity and sleep, closing for several seconds and then opening with effort.

"It's the age-old story, isn't it, Aaron? We struggle each day with the dichotomy, the balance between the undeniable knowledge that we are only a tiny, insignificant clan of watery creatures on a little lost planet in endless infinite black space, destined to die and be forgotten for eternity, compared to the unbreakable faith that we are in fact God's children, the chosen ones, making important decisions and embracing the miracle of our existence, honoring the gift by living the good man's life, finding a grain of worthiness in every hopeless minute."

As he had before, Bryan leaned forward and crossed his arms on the wooden table, lowering his weary head to rest in the cradle he created. A few minutes passed, and I made the decision to leave him alone.

Before I moved, Bryan, with his face still nestled in the warmth of his pale sweater, said softly, "I don't know what will happen tomorrow."

At the time, it struck me as extremely profound. Like it should be the line carved on each of our headstones. The last thing anyone says to anybody, instead of "Goodbye" or "I love you" or "Go to hell."

I walked back to my room down the long, hollow hallway. My hand fished deep in my front pocket for the key the Mongolian gave me earlier. Before I could pull the key from my pocket, there was a strange sound behind me, followed immediately by a tremendous sharp sting on the back of my neck.

"Shit," I yelled, and put my fingers to the spot expecting blood. Looking down at my clean hand, I said "Shit" again, less loudly, but equally meaningful, mostly to myself.

Down at the far end of the hall stood a figure in the semi-darkness, petite, dressed all in bright blue and wearing some sort of mask. The person held a rifle up to their shoulder pointed directly at me, and before I could say "Shit" a third time, there was the sound of pressurized air bursting from the barrel, and I was stung in the middle of my forehead by another buzzing pellet. It was fucking unbelievable.

"Jesus Christ," I yelled, reaching for the new injury. "Stop," I said, covering my eyes and turning my back to the maniac in blue.

The gun was still pointed in my direction. There was a spot of blood on my finger from the forehead shot. I imagined a tiny crimson line to the middle of my eyes.

"I know it's you, Lei. Stop."

It had to be her. Petite, standing directly in front of the room where I'd seen her before. The blue outfit appeared oriental, a pointed collar. Even the Mardi Gras mask had an Asian look. She hated me, wanted me gone, hadn't even come to dinner.

She pulled the trigger again. I felt the sting on my back through the shirt, quick and painful like a dart. And then again on the hip, not so bad through the pants.

"Ahhh. Stop, damn it."

I reached in my pocket for the key and began fumbling at the lock. Another shot, the pop of air and the pain under my arm. The key in the lock, the door open, a final shot ricocheting against the frame and down the corridor.

I slammed the door and locked it behind me. The peephole was empty. The assault was over, like a nightmare movie sequence, shot five times in the hallway by a masked pellet-gunman. How long had she waited for me there, gun ready at her shoulder?

I examined my wounds in the mirror. The bump on my forehead was red and swollen, grown to the circumference of a dime. It was truly unbelievable.

I was afraid to leave the room. There was no one to call. The Mongolian? Bryan? Little Doctor Lambert?

I took a shower to cleanse myself from the day's travels, the uncertainty. Before climbing into bed, I pushed a chair up against the doorknob.

The wine, Bryan's prophecy, the attack in the hallway, and the decision I would announce the following morning kept me awake. Not to mention the swing vote. There was simply no point in closing my eyes. I stared at the ceiling in the darkness and then I heard the softest of knocks on the door.

I recognized that knock. Adrianna. I crept quietly to the door and peered through the peephole.

There she stood, in a simple yellow dress, hair pulled back. I couldn't see her feet but somehow knew they were bare. She seemed sad, leaning forward and knocking softly again. Beautiful and brown. I could see her eyes.

I pulled away from the peephole and leaned my back against the side wall.

In a low voice, I heard Adrianna whisper, "Aaron, let me in. I need to tell you something. It's important."

Frozen with uncertainty, I just stayed where I was.

She knocked lightly a third time.

"Please," she whispered. "I need to tell you something."

But I didn't move. Just stood in my underwear, back against the wall, until I heard Adrianna's bare feet move away down the hall. I still wonder what she came to tell me, and whether it might have changed the unforgettable events of the next day.

At nine fifty the Mongolian knocked hard on my door. Through the peephole I could see his unmistakable rigid figure. As I stared at the man, I thought again of the government soldiers rushing into the city from the surrounding woods, taking all of us into custody, holding us in small groups behind chain-link fences. We'd be removed one by one for interrogation. The Mongolian wouldn't say a word, hard and resolute, the personification of justified revolution. I, on the other hand, would continue to scream, "I never committed."

The time had come. I opened the door. The Mongolian's eyes were instantly drawn to the dime-sized red dot in the center of my forehead.

"You wouldn't believe what happened to me last night," I said.

The Mongolian turned to lead me down the hallway. I caught up and continued my explanation unasked.

"I got ambushed right here in the hallway. I was on the way back from dinner. Before I could get in the door, someone opened fire on me with a damn pellet gun."

The Mongolian glanced up, his eyes returning to my forehead. He radiated disbelief.

"It's true," I said. "She shot me at least five times before I could get away. I've got a welt on my damn neck the size of a grape. Look!"

I pulled my collar to the side, but the Mongolian wasn't paying attention, busy escorting me to the Committee Chamber for my grand appearance. He probably didn't believe me anyway. Why should he?

"I think it was Lei," I mumbled. "Why would she do it? What could she possibly accomplish?"

The Mongolian broke his silence. "You're an idiot," he said plainly.

I was taken aback by the fact he had spoken at all, and also unsure how to respond. As usual, the halls were long and empty, the walls mostly bare, the doors all closed.

I reached into my pants pocket and felt something smooth, the size of a silver dollar but fatter. I pulled it out to see the wishing bean. It wasn't possible the bean was in my pants all along. I'd given it to Sara. It was stolen. Was it a different bean? When was the last time I'd worn these pants?

We reached the entrance to the Committee Chamber. The Mongolian checked his silver watch and stood facing the door.

I suddenly felt overwhelmingly anxious. I'd made up my mind through the sleepless night, but the decision didn't seem to calm my nerves. I'd rehearsed the words over and over, carefully chosen, and now I stood with the Mongolian at the entrance to the vast Committee Chamber, unprepared for the intimidation.

I said to the back of the Mongolian's head, "The thing with the cat was an accident. It was nobody's fault."

There was a peculiar period of silence, and then the big doors opened from the inside.

The enormous room was larger than in my imagination. The seven pedestals were empty. Only one of the tables in the inner circle was occupied. The black man in the grey suit sat quietly at the same table as before, his head bent slightly over paperwork stacked neatly in front of him.

I was lead by the Mongolian to the table where Gary Jones had been before. The black man never looked up from his papers. I noticed his fingernails were perfect, trimmed and shaped.

The Mongolian took a seat at the third table, folding his meaty hands in front of him. His expression revealed nothing, just as I imagined he would sit in the room with the government agents as they tried their interrogation tricks. Bright lights, promises of cool water—nothing would break the rock-solid Mongolian.

Somewhere in a distant chamber a clock struck ten. On the tenth chime, I heard a door open. In sequence the Committee members took their seats looking down on me. First Luke, then Lei, Abdul, Bryan, Larry, Ivan, and finally Adrianna.

Like a defendant in a courtroom facing the verdict, I watched each Committee member to see if they'd meet my eyes, but none so much as glanced in my direction. Even Adrianna looked directly at the well-dressed black man, who rose from his chair to address the assembly.

I knew I was specially set on the agenda. In my mind I expected the well-dressed man to announce the purpose of our meeting, the declaration of my decision, and then I expected the opportunity to stand and address the Committee, hoping my rehearsed words would come easy. Afterward, I wasn't sure exactly what to expect, but I felt prepared one way or the other.

I was wrong.

The well-dressed man began to speak. "We are here today concerning Mr. Aaron Jennings." His pronunciation of the words was as perfect as his fingernails. His mouth moved carefully. "There have been serious allegations waged against Mr. Jennings. Among these allegations, he is specifically accused of violating the provisions of Article 9 of the *Manifesto*, the capital offense of distortion of our history by those who document such things."

I was dumbstruck. In the silence that followed, after the initial shock, there was the fleeting thought it was all a joke. A big joke, probably Bryan's idea, and any minute they would all burst into laughter. But nobody laughed.

Sitting third from my left, at Bryan's right-hand side, Abdul, the sleepy, quiet, spiritual Muslim, stood defiantly. He held a document up to his face, shifted his glasses and read, "The details of the allegations against Mr. Jennings are as follows. Number one: Mr. Jennings has lied and deceived this Committee concerning his actions leading to the death and subsequent burning of Adrianna's bird."

I looked at Adrianna. Her head was down. Luke simply watched Abdul speak, co-conspirators in whatever was happening to me.

"Number two: Mr. Jennings has demonstrated his disloyalty in concealing the fact that he was approached on at least two occasions by someone he believed to be a United States Government agent attempting to recruit him in an effort to undermine the Jamestown movement."

My eyes flew to Bryan. His haggard face could barely hold my gaze, but he didn't look away.

The Muslim continued with subtle pleasure, "Number three: Mr. Jennings has violated his marital vows to his wife and God by committing adultery during his visit to the new city."

I put my hand to my face and rubbed my own tired eyes. What had Adrianna come to tell me the night before? I felt the wishing bean in my pocket, smooth and reassuring, but empty of wishes. I'd used my only wish on a plane destined not to crash anyway.

"Number four: Mr. Jennings continued his pattern of deception and dishonesty by denying to our Committee Chairman he'd had contact with any Committee member during his recent stay at home."

I could feel the internal shift from bewilderment to a slow escalation of absolute and total anger.

"And lastly, the most serious of the allegations. Number five: Mr. Jennings is accused of the capital offense of compromising history by brokering an agreement with a Committee member, whereby Mr. Jennings would agree to distort the truth in exchange for the specific Committee member accepting responsibility for something Mr. Jennings himself had done."

I removed my hand from my face in time to see Abdul raise his head from the document and look down at me over his glasses like I was the vilest specimen he had ever viewed from his lofty perch in the Committee ring.

I no longer held any expectations. I stood to defend myself before any invitation was extended. The Mongolian stood at the same time like a bouncer at a bar, arms crossed over his chest.

All the words I'd memorized were gone.

"Fuck you people," I finally yelled. More like a blast of frustration than an actual sentence. "I'm being judged by complete freaks. All of you."

I was out of order. Disrespectful to the insane process. The Mongolian started around the table in my direction. Before he got halfway, Bryan raised his hand. The Mongolian stopped on command, holding his position.

With my newfound freedom to speak, I raised my arms.

"Look at yourselves. Each one of you. Eaten up with weakness like cancer."

I turned to Larry.

"You're crazy with envy. Hated me the first time you laid eyes on me. Admit it. And what the hell is with the chef's hat? Are you a cartoon character?"

I pointed at Ivan and yelled, "Bigfoot's not real, you stupid bastard. The body they found in Oregon was a hoax. A frozen gorilla suit. And by the way, you've got a chip on your shoulder bigger than your head. You're pissed off all the time. You hate Luke because he was born with money and you weren't."

From so far away I could hear the big, sweaty Russian breathing through his hair-filled nose, but he didn't move a muscle.

"Abdul. I don't know what to say about you. You sleep all the time, and then you seem to enjoy my demise. You're supposed to be a man of God. Is it godly to look down at another man the way you look down at me? To find pleasure in another's misfortune?"

I skipped left to point at Luke. "And you, Luke. What a pussy you are. So full of pride. You put yourself ahead of everything. Everybody else. Jamestown. The Committee." I shook my head and continued, "And what in the hell happened to make you feel the urge to cut your own ass with a pocket knife until it bleeds?" I yelled, arms outstretched. "I saw it. I saw the blood."

The anger in my chest boiled out my mouth. My mind was cleansing itself, but I wasn't finished yet. My eyes scanned the circle and stopped on Lei.

"Lei, the Asian, lesbian, genius, swing vote. Rancid with jealousy. Can't even see straight.

"And would you please explain what you expected to accomplish by shooting me with a pellet gun in the hall last night? Look at my forehead, you crazy bitch. It still hurts. I think the pellet lodged inside."

I pulled my bangs back, the skin tight, and touched the red dot with my index finger. Lei had a look of fear, terrified by the mere confrontation. For a moment I doubted she was the shooter.

I looked at Adrianna. Her head was still down. There was nothing left. Eventually my eyes came to rest on Bryan.

"And you," I said. "Bryan. The man who shows up in my house one morning. The man who pops pain pills like they're candy and criticizes the drug addicts. Sleeps with Rita Blanchard and curses adulterers. Lies to the liars, deceives the deceivers, but he's always got a nice, new sweater.

"You're the worst of them all. The biggest hypocrite in the circle, but I think you already knew that, didn't you?"

The cavernous Committee Chamber fell silent with my final words. For at least thirty seconds no one moved and no one spoke. It felt like longer. I wasn't sure whether to sit down or walk away.

In a tone I hadn't heard before, resigned yet almost whimsical, Bryan's voice said, "You're right, we're all sinners. Rife with weakness."

He sighed, "There are no 'great' people. It's a myth. A myth we created to separate ourselves. We all eat, drink, crap, and cry. We're all created in the same dark hole, and we'll all die."

Bryan paused, and then followed the pause with a question. "Do you know what the difference is between us and you?"

I waited a sufficient amount of time. "No, what's the difference, Bryan?"

"Nothing," he said.

We were left again with the hellish silence.

Bryan said softly, "The only people who can break your heart are the ones you let hold it in their hands."

I was suddenly exhausted, a wave of anemia trickling through my bones. I was tired of trying to figure out his point.

The man in the neat grey suit stood.

Bryan asked, "What say you, Mr. Bass?"

The black man spoke again. "Accusation Number Five states that Mr. Jennings is guilty of 'distortion of our history by those who document such things.' Although he failed to deny any of the allegations against him, Mr. Jennings is not officially deemed the person to document our history. He cannot be found guilty of a capital offense in my opinion. Mr. Jennings can, of course, be expelled by a majority vote of this Committee for any of the reasons previously set forth."

Larry said, "I make a motion for the Committee to vote on the permanent expulsion of Aaron Jennings from Jamestown."

Luke said, "I second the motion. The subject needs to step out of the room for the taking of the vote."

I probably should have walked away, gotten my luggage, and left without a thought to how the Committee voted, but instead, I refused to leave.

"I'm not going."

The Mongolian, frothing at the mouth to beat my ass, made another move in my direction. This time Bryan stopped him with his words.

"Very well. All those in favor of the permanent expulsion of Aaron Jennings, raise your hands when called upon."

Bryan started at his far right, pointing at Luke. Luke raised his hand without hesitation.

Bryan moved his finger to Lei, the next in line. She raised her hand. And then Abdul, Bryan, Larry, and Ivan all raised their grimy hands.

Finally, it was Adrianna's turn. She didn't move right away. Slumped down in her chair, eyes at a downward angle, there was a moment of hope, but then the moment was dashed. Adrianna raised her pretty brown hand.

The energy was completely gone from my body. I remember being told to get up. I remember the wishing bean smooth in my hand, and then refusing to move from my chair. And lastly, I remember an ass-kicking from my old friend, the mad Mongolian, like I hadn't had since elementary school.

THE CONCLUSION

I woke up in the backseat of a car I later learned would deliver me to the nearest commercial airport. I flew back home without one-legged birds, or pilots with chef's hats, or miniature doctors handing out magic beans. It was uneventful, so there was plenty of time to think about the past weeks.

I borrowed a pen from the stewardess and began taking notes in the margins of a magazine. The ideas flowed freely and didn't stop until I arrived home. I made deadline with the editor, and *Jamestown, Alaska* became my best-selling book by far. Ultimately, as you've seen, it wasn't written in eight parts as I originally envisioned. Instead, I wrote the story from my own perspective and called it a novel. Changed a few names, altered a few descriptions.

Years after my final visit to Alaska, during my promotional tour at a book signing in St. Paul, Minnesota, I looked up to see Bryan standing in front of me. He was the last person in line, his sweater brown this time, looking at least ten years older than he looked when last I'd seen him above me in the Committee Chamber. He was holding a copy of my book and handed it to me.

Bryan said, "There is a time in every man's education when he arrives at the conviction that envy is ignorance, that imitation is suicide."

There was a moment between us. We were very much alone in the crowded room.

"I know that one," I said. "It's Emerson."

His face revealed satisfaction.

"Very good."

There were people around us, but they were all paying attention to other things. We were able to hold a private conversation in the middle of the store.

I opened his book to the proper page for an inscription and a sweeping signature.

"You changed a few things in there," he said, motioning to the book in my hands.

I nodded my head.

"I never had sex with a woman named Rita Blanchard," Bryan said, and smiled enough to lighten the situation.

I began to write in his book, careful not to make a mistake.

Bryan continued, "We're all messed up, Aaron. Every one of us. No exceptions. All flawed, susceptible to weakness by definition."

I couldn't tell if he wanted my approval or just needed to give an explanation. He seemed worn out.

I finished the inscription and handed Bryan his book, hoping he'd walk away and see what I'd written at a later time. Instead, he stood before me and read my words out loud.

"The greatest ideas in the history of the human mind are crushed under the weight of the humanity itself."

He kept his eyes on the page after he'd finished, reading the sentence again silently. A lady got in line behind Bryan, peering around him to see the cause of the delay.

"You gave up you too quickly, Aaron," he said softly. "Too easily."

I said, "There is no solution, Bryan. There's never been a solution, and there never will be. And you know why? In order to find a solution, we have to first identify the problem, and the problem remains that humans are human and cannot become something else. That's it. That's all there is."

I expected a comment in return, a lucid argument, another quote. With no expression on his face, Bryan closed his book, turned around, and walked away. Watching him go reminded me of the first day we met, the morning on the porch when Bryan left me alone and walked slowly through my backyard, stopping briefly on the worn patch of earth next to the trampoline. He moved with gentle purpose.

I never saw or heard from Bryan again.

When Sara turned fifteen, she begged to read *Jamestown*. I finally relented, figuring she'd heard and seen worse things on television every night than she'd read in my book. But I feared Sara would be unable to separate me from the novel. Unable to divide fiction from the bits of truth.

Coming home to my wife and children was no compromise, even if Michelle would never love me the way she had before. The story of Jamestown was so wild and interesting nobody believed for a minute it was true, and to be honest, this many years later, I can barely tell the difference myself.

"Dad," Sara asked after she finished the book, "was there really an Adrianna?"

"No," I answered. "It's just a story."

"But I remember you giving me the wishing bean, and I remember George."

"Whatever happened to George?" I asked, steering the conversation.

"I don't know. He moved away. He never really liked me, you know. He just acted like he did so I'd give him the chips from my lunch every day. Mom packed good chips."

She'd grown into a beautiful young woman. We were still best friends, and we usually found the time each morning to sit at the breakfast table together for a few minutes like we'd always done.

"Why didn't it work?" she asked. "The Alaska idea?"

"Well," I said, "like so many grand ideas, it was only grand from a distance, and we don't have the benefit of distance. Do we?"

"I still think it could work," she said.

Sara was on the backside of the awkward years. I could still see the little girl in her face, but there was no denying she'd leave me in a few short years.

She asked, "Have you met the new neighbors?"

"New neighbors?"

"Yeah. Across the street. They started moving in their stuff Saturday when you were out of town."

"Across the street?" I asked.

The Matsons' house had been empty since Mr. Matson supposedly died of a heart attack. I went to the funeral, but it was a closed casket, so I never actually saw the body.

After Sara went to school, and Michelle and Brad left me alone in the house, I stood at the front window in my white robe, naked underneath, sipping warm coffee from my favorite mug.

It was a clear day, the sun bright on the manicured green lawns and the hot cement of the road between my window and the Matsons' old house. It was dark behind me, and I counted on the contrast to make me mostly invisible.

Something caught my eye in the front window on the other side of the street. Just the slightest movement, a change in coloration, grey to grey.

I stared at the window, and as I stared, the figure of a man slowly came into focus. A man standing at the window, perhaps also counting on the darkness in the room behind him to make his body invisible.

But I could see him, the outline of the broad shoulders, the head tilted just a bit, arms at his sides, watching me watching. And the longer I stared, the more I became convinced the man in the window was the Mongolian, barrel-chested and silent, watching, tracking every move I made.

"Shit," I said.

ACKNOWLEDGMENTS

Mom and Skip, Dad and Jan, Allison, Dusty, Mary Grace, Lilly, Demi, Steadman, Barry Munday, Michelle Dotter, Delilah and Joey, Steve Gillis, Joel Stabler, Guy Intoci, Sonny Brewer, Angie Kaiser, Mike and Sharon, Rodney and Roni, Paige and Tommy, Ellen and Bob, Bill and Linda, Page and Palette Bookstore, Bluto and the Boys, Kyle Jennings, Jim Gilbert, Smokey Davis, and probably all sorts of other people that I forgot to mention who deserve thanks for all their support.

ABOUT THE AUTHOR

Frank Turner Hollon is the author of ten novels, two of which were adapted to film: *Blood and Circumstance* and *Life Is a Strange Place*, which was released under the title *Barry Munday*. Hollon practices law in Alabama and lives in Robertsdale, AL.